# Little Hornet
## Boy Patriot of North Carolina

## Patriot Kids of the
## American Revolution Series

## Book One

GEOFF BAGGETT

# DEDICATION

To our kids.  They need to know and connect with their history.   I hope that my stories will help them make a connection.

# CHAPTER ONE

A loud gunshot snatched William Hamilton from his happy, deep sleep. Something was shaking his leg, too. He opened his eyes and saw his big brother, James, holding his finger up to his lips.

William was a little confused. For a moment he couldn't remember where he was. Then he realized that he was sleeping in Mrs. Mary Kate McClelland's barn. The Hamilton brothers had traveled down from their home near Charlotte, North Carolina, to help the widow lady on her farm. So her barn was their temporary bedroom.

The Revolutionary War had come to South Carolina in the spring of 1780, and Charlestown had fallen to the Redcoats in May. Tory and British soldiers now roamed the countryside, taking supplies from the farms and causing a lot of trouble for Patriot families.

Mrs. McClelland's husband had died during one of the British raids into the Waxhaws. Her two oldest sons had been captured at Charlestown and were being held on prison ships in the harbor there. This poor widow owned a big farm and had a house full of small children to care for. That's why the Hamilton brothers were in South Carolina ... to deliver a generous collection of gifts, food, and clothes from their church and to work on the widow's farm for a few days.

So far it had been a wonderful trip. William was having the adventure of a lifetime. He made lots of new friends. He taught the little McClelland boys, David and James, how to chop weeds from their cornfield. He even took them hunting and got a deer. They roasted the meat over a fire and had it for supper. It fed the whole family and all of the guests!

But now, in the middle of the night, something was very wrong. William could tell by the look on his big brother's face.

James hissed in the darkness, "Shhh … Be quiet, William."

"What's wrong, James?"

"I heard a gunshot and breaking glass. And I think I heard someone scream. Something's not right."

William looked around in the darkness of the hayloft where the boys had been sleeping. His other big brother, John, was awake. So was Andy Jackson, a neighbor of the McClelland family and a new friend that they had made on their trip to South Carolina.

The boys all crawled to the loft window and carefully peered over the rough sill. In the clearing beside the house stood three men in strange green uniforms holding torches and pointing muskets at a sobbing huddle of terrified children. Through the tiny window of the cabin they saw flames dancing. There was more breaking glass. They heard the horrible sound of screams coming from behind the house.

"Those are British Legion dragoons!" hissed Andy. "They're Colonel Banastre Tarleton's men, Tories from up north. I can tell by the green coats. What are they doing this far from Charlestown?"

A frightened scream emanated from the darkness.

"That's Margaret, for sure. It sounds like she's out back!" exclaimed James in an excited whisper. His voice was filled with fear and rage.

Margaret McClelland was the oldest daughter of the Mrs. McClelland. James Hamilton had fallen in love with her the moment that he saw her three days ago. Just the night before he had asked her to marry him. And she said, "Yes." Margaret McClelland was going to be James Hamilton's wife.

"I don't see Mrs. McClelland. And it looks one of the boys is missing. I can't tell which one," added John.

"I've got to go help Margaret!" James headed for the cluster of flintlocks standing in the corner.

"James, you can't go charging with guns blazing into a bunch of armed militia. It's too dangerous," cautioned John. "You need to think before you act."

More screams filled the night. Frantic. Wailing. Piercing.

James rapidly assessed the situation and then voiced his plan. "I'm going to work my way through the trees around back of the house. I'm going to fight off any militiamen that I see back there. I want you boys to get your guns and take aim at those three soldiers who are guarding the McClelland kids. The second you hear me start shooting I want you to shoot those Tories."

"All right, James, but what then?" asked John.

James wrapped his belt around his waist, sticking his sheathed knife inside the leather on his left hip, then replied, "If you don't see any more soldiers after a while, come on down and check out the cabin, and then work your way around back and find me."

James prepared to drop through the ladder hole to the barn floor below. "Good luck, boys. Don't get shot," he cautioned. Then he was gone.

John, Andy, and William retrieved their guns and shooting bags from the corner and made their way toward the window.

"Are you boys all loaded?" asked John.

"Yes," replied William.

"Always," answered Andy.

"Make sure your frizzen cover is off and that you have a good pile of powder in your pan. We want all of these shots to go off like they're supposed to," urged John.

John stepped up to the window to take another look at the Tory guards. They were still standing watch over the kids. All three had their backs to the barn.

"I'm going to take the one on the left. William, you take the one in the middle. Andy, you take the one on the right. Let's go ahead and line up the shots. Nothing fancy. Aim dead center of the middle of the back. It won't take James too long to work his way around back of the house, so we need to be ready," stated John.

The boys stood well inside the room with their barrels resting on the high sill of the opening. It was a perfect height for Andy and William. John had to spread his legs a bit to stand comfortably and not hunch over.

"I don't like this," whined William. "Those are men down there. Not rabbits or deer. And we're going to shoot them? It just doesn't seem right."

"Those Tories are aiming muskets at some little kids … our friends, William," retorted Andy. "They are enemy soldiers, and this is a war. We have to fight back."

"He's right, William. Nobody makes war on a house full of women and children. What these Tories are doing is not right. Tonight justice is up to us. Now make ready, boys."

Two long rifles and William's stubby musket issued a subtle "crack" as the boys pulled the hammers back to full cock.

"Sight in on your man," John ordered. "Now we wait."

The boys waited for only a few minutes, but it seemed like an eternity to them.

The sudden crack of the gunshot from behind the cabin startled all three of the boys, shaking them from their concentration upon their targets. The three soldiers guarding the children jumped as well, instinctively lifting their weapons toward the sound of the shot.

"Fire!" yelled John.

He and Andy fired their rifles simultaneously. William's shot was about a half-second behind theirs. All three bullets found their marks. Two of the soldiers fell. The middle one stumbled forward, spun around, and shot back at the barn. The Tory then took off running for cover behind the house. John reloaded his flintlock quickly and fired again. The enemy soldier went down. The yard became suddenly quiet.

Andy, finished with his reloading, replaced his ramrod, cocked his rifle, and trained his sites on the cabin door. William fell down on his knees, spun around and sat against the wall, and burst into hysterical tears. He covered his face with his hands.

"I'm sorry, Johnny! I'm so sorry, Johnny! I didn't mean to miss my shot. I swear, Johnny! I had my sites right on him! I don't know what happened."

John sought to console him as he reloaded. "You didn't miss, William. You hit him. It's going to be all right. You did what you had to do."

William refused to be consoled. He wept silently.

John rejoined Andy in the window with his rifle freshly loaded. "See anything, Andy?"

"No. Nothing's moving as far as I can tell. Those kids are probably scattered all in the woods. I'll bet they're still running. We need to go down and check on James and see if we can find the kids and get them inside."

John and Andy exited the barn cautiously. They aimed their rifles left and right, prepared for possible enemy soldiers concealed in the woods. They saw no one. Even better, no one shot at them.

"I'll go look for the little ones," Andy volunteered.

John barked an order to William, hiding in the cover of the barn, "William, you go around back and check on James. But be careful! Don't shoot at anything you can't see. Stay in the shadows. And whatever you do, don't shoot James!"

William wiped the tears from his eyes with his shirtsleeve. "All right, Johnny."

William ran out of the door of the barn. He trotted to the right, skirting the edge of the trees, and headed for the clearing behind the cabin. What he found there was the saddest thing he ever saw. James was sitting on the ground and holding his fiancé, Margaret, in his arms. His big brother was sobbing.

William cried out, "Johnny! Come quick!"

# CHAPTER TWO

William came to a decision as he jostled about in the seat of the wagon. He never wanted to shoot another man. Ever.

He thought, "I'm just as much a Patriot as my brothers, but I don't ever want to see anything like that again."

The boys were headed back home to Mecklenburg County, North Carolina. William was driving the Hamilton wagon westward out of the village of Lancaster. His brothers trusted him to drive their wagon. William loved guiding a team of horses. He was good at it.

He was quickly becoming a man on the Carolina frontier. After all, he had just recently turned thirteen years old. He could work on the farm, drive a wagon, hunt, and fish like any grown man. He even worked in his stepfather's salt mining operation. Yes, William Hamilton was becoming a fine, hard-working young man.

And he understood what was happening in the world around him ... how so many people in the colonies wanted to be free from the rule of England and King George III. But he was having a lot of trouble understanding what had happened two nights ago at the McClelland farm.

Why would soldiers want to harm women and children? What did that have to do with the war for independence? How could people be so cruel to others? It just wasn't fair!

Those soldiers had been very cruel, indeed, on that dark, scary night. It just didn't make any sense. Three members of the McClelland family died in the attack. The poor widow McClelland and her little boy, Jacob, had been found in the cabin. And then there was Margaret. She died in James Hamilton's arms.

William would never forget how his brother cried out and wept. He had never seen a man cry like that. It was so very sad. The day before the attack James had been making plans for his wedding to Margaret. But then one day later he stood by her graveside for her funeral.

And then there were the Tory militiamen. Five green-coated soldiers of the British Legion rode onto the McClelland farm that night. Because of what James, John, Andy Jackson, and William did, none of them ever left that farm. The Patriot militia buried the men on the hillside above the cabin on the morning after the raid.

William shuddered at the thought of it. He pulled the collar of his wool coat up under his chin to help ward off the cool air. He snapped the reins and clucked at the horses to encourage them along the rutted roadway.

They had about seven miles to travel before reaching the northward highway that would take them back into Mecklenburg County. William pushed the team hard, hoping to make it back into North Carolina before nightfall.

The road was muddy, but not impassable, and they made steady progress. At one point they had to cross a small creek. The water was over a foot deep and flowing vigorously because of recent heavy rains. William talked softly to the team and made the crossing carefully and slowly.

The miles passed quietly. About an hour after noon

they approached a small rise in the road. As they neared the hilltop they heard shouts, clanking metal sounds, creaking wagons, and the snorts of horses far off to their right. The sounds grew louder.

"We must be near the crossroad," observed John. "It sure sounds busy on the northern road, doesn't it?"

"A little too busy," mused James.

When they topped the hill they saw the source of all of the noise and activity. A large convoy of wagons and men was approaching steadily from the south. There were several hundred men accompanying the wagons, some on horseback, but most on foot. Most of the men wore blue and red Continental Army uniforms.

"Those are Continentals!" exclaimed John. "But I thought they were all captured at Charlestown."

"It looks like they didn't catch them all," commented James. "They're moving pretty fast and yelling a lot. Must be in a hurry. I don't want to be in front of this bunch, for sure. They'll push us too hard. We'll just wait here at this crossroad and let them pass, then we can follow at our own pace."

William eased the team to a stop about fifty yards short of the intersection. John broke out a sack full of snacks and passed them around for a makeshift meal. A cluster of five officers soon broke away from the head of the column and trotted across the field toward their wagon. It appeared that the column was stopping. Men were dismounting and almost everyone began to sit down along the side of the road to rest.

"We've got company coming, boys," commented James.

They waited as the officers trotted up to the Hamilton wagon.

"Good day to you, gentlemen," one of the officers spoke. He was a kindly looking middle-aged fellow.

"I'm Colonel Abraham Buford of the Third Virginia Regiment and in command of this detachment. I trust you boys are not of a loyalist persuasion."

"You would be right, sir. I'm James Hamilton, private in the Mecklenburg County Militia of North Carolina. These are my brothers John and William."

"Outstanding! Are you in this area on official business for the military?" inquired the colonel.

"No, sir," responded James. "We had some personal business down here in the Waxhaws for a few days, but now we're heading home. We thought that we might wait here for a while and let you gentlemen pass and then fall in behind you."

"I thought all the Continentals surrendered at Charlestown," interjected John. "How did you avoid capture?"

The colonel smiled. "Well, son, we were not at Charlestown for the surrender, thank God! I was dispatched there to bring relief to the siege, but we arrived too late. We are returning to North Carolina to regroup with our forces there, but the British have been dogging us for days. General Lord Cornwallis is now out of Charlestown and seeking to subdue the countryside. Have you gentlemen seen any sign of the enemy?"

"We encountered a few of them night before last. Five men of the British Legion a few miles west of here," responded James.

"That is our nemesis, for sure! Loyalist cavalry and dragoons under the command of Colonel Banastre Tarleton. They have pursued us for days. It must have been one of his forward patrols," observed the colonel.

"Well, these men attacked a helpless family that night near Lancaster. We happened to be staying on the farm, sleeping in the barn. We killed them all, but not before they murdered two women and a child."

"Absolutely horrible, but not surprising," commented the Colonel, shaking his head. "These beasts are unleashing many such horrors upon the people of South Carolina. They must be driven back into the sea."

"Sir, look! An enemy soldier under white flag of truce!" exclaimed one of the other officers.

# CHAPTER THREE

A lone rider dressed in the unmistakable bright green and red of the British Legion rode rapidly along the road beside the column.

William thought, "He looks exactly like the men we fought at the farm!" He was frightened.

The enemy soldier paused briefly, then following the directions of several finger-pointing men, galloped across the short grass toward the officers gathered around the Hamilton wagon. He yanked the reins and pulled to a rapid halt twenty feet away. He arrogantly sized up the gathering of officers before him.

"Whom, may I ask, is the officer commanding this column?" he inquired with a thick, educated British accent.

"That would be me, Lieutenant. Colonel Abraham Buford, Third Virginia Regiment, representing the Continental Congress of the United States of America, in command of this column and detachment. State your business, son."

"Colonel, I am Lieutenant Andrew Mayfair of the British Legion, at your service. I bear a message from Colonel Banastre Tarleton, commandant of the Legion."

"What is Tarleton's message, young man?"

"Sir, the commandant wishes me to inform you that you are now surrounded by seven hundred troops on horseback. We also have infantry and cannons. General Lord Cornwallis is approaching and only a short distance away. The commandant urges that you surrender immediately to avoid more bloodshed."

One of the worried-looking officers spoke up, "Perhaps we should surrender, Colonel. It sounds as if there is a formidable force arrayed against us."

The colonel ignored him, peering at the messenger. Fishing for more information, he asked, "Seven hundred men, you say? Not likely! And you say Cornwallis is close by? How close?"

"I can offer no other comment, sir. I am only authorized to deliver the commandant's terms ... nothing more. And I am to await your response."

The Patriot officers stared expectantly at the face of their colonel. At long last he spoke, "You may deliver the following message to your commandant, Lieutenant.

*"Sir, I reject your proposals, and shall defend myself to the last extremity."*

"As you wish," the officer countered snidely. "By your leave."

He spun his horse on its heels and galloped southward. His white flag danced in the soft breeze.

The colonel addressed his officers, "Fifteen more minutes of rest, men, and then we proceed northward. I do not believe a single word of that pompous brat, but we still need to move quickly."

"Yes, sir," a major responded. "Gentlemen ..." The officers tipped their hats at the Hamilton brothers. "Good luck."

James spoke, "Well, Colonel, it looks like we're in for a fight. We'll go ahead and fall in with your boys."

The officer shook his head. "No, son. This is not your fight. I want you to move on. Three more muskets won't make a difference if Tarleton has the numbers of men that he claims to have. Besides, you will better serve the cause by going ahead to Charlotte and warning them about the British move out of Charlestown."

The colonel pointed to a tree-covered ridge about a half-mile to the northwest. "You boys need to get moving now and get under cover of those trees. If there is action, it will be in this open field here near this crossroad. You should be safe up there. Once there is no danger of pursuit, proceed northward."

"Are you sure, Colonel? We don't want to run from a fight."

"Private!" the colonel barked. "Do not question my orders. Get your brothers under cover and then deliver the news of this British incursion to Charlotte and areas northward. Do I make myself clear?"

"Yes, sir."

The colonel extended his hand to James. "Good luck, Mr. Hamilton. And God speed." He turned his horse and trotted back toward the column of Continentals.

"You heard him, boys, let's hit the tree line," muttered James.

William clucked at his team and popped the reins, slowly leading the wagon onto the highway northward. The road was horribly thick with mud, but they managed to cover a half-mile in about thirty minutes.

William guided the horses off of the road and sought refuge in the trees. He hid the wagon and team behind a small knoll, next to a depression with ample water for the horses. The boys dismounted, stretched their muscles, and took a drink of water themselves. William grabbed a sack of corn to feed the horses a meal. James and John sat down against an oak tree, watching the Continentals in the clearing to their south.

"James, do you reckon there's a big fight coming?" asked William.

"I assume so. Sounds like that Colonel Tarleton is aching for one."

"Will we be safe up here?" William sounded worried.

"Oh, sure. We'll be fine up here. We even have a first class seat to watch the whole show." James smiled at his little brother. "Don't you worry, tadpole, I won't let those green coats get hold of you. "

"James, the column is back on the move," interrupted John. "And I see riders way off on that far ridge! Look! There's smoke way down the road!"

Seconds later the muffled crack of musket fire reached their ears. There were six or seven shots, followed by silence.

"What happened, James?" William asked. "Was that it? Was that the battle?"

"No … that was likely just the rear guard. That was a long way down the road from the sound of it. They were probably shooting to warn Colonel Buford. But, really, there's no way to tell."

The boys watched the action unfolding below. The wagons moved northward along the road while the infantry fanned out into a single line on both sides of the muddy trail. Riders in dark green uniforms came over the far ridge and began forming up, as well. There were three separate groups of them. They looked to be about three hundred yards out from the Continentals.

Moments later the cavalrymen on the right flank began their charge toward the Continentals, led by a flashy officer who was vigorously waving his sword in the air.

"That has to be Colonel Tarleton," commented James. "That feisty fellow over on the right flank. Do you see him?"

"I see him," responded William. "He's sure putting on a show, isn't he?"

The other groups of green-clad horsemen followed the Colonel's enthusiastic charge. They all converged upon the line of foot soldiers. It took a couple of seconds before the thunder or their hooves traveled across the expanse of the field and reached the boys' ears. The horses increased in speed as they continued down the hill. They were almost upon the Patriots.

"Why aren't they firing? They're right on top of them!" wailed William.

The smoke of the first shots erupted as William's final word still hung in the air, followed by the echo of their explosions. There was one modest volley of musket fire from the Continentals, but that was all. Colonel Tarleton and several of his men on the right went down hard, their horses apparently shot from beneath them. They couldn't tell if the Colonel had been hit because of the volume of smoke hovering over the field.

Suddenly William saw movement to the left as a handful of riders emerged from the smoke. They were leaning low over their mounts and galloping hard toward the woods to the east of the boys' position.

"Isn't that Colonel Buford?" asked William.

"Yep. That's Buford. And most of his staff, it looks like. Cowards!" James spat on the ground. "I reckon the boys of the Third Virginia are on their own now."

Screams continued to emanate from the battlefield. Men on horseback rode to and fro, swinging their swords in high, powerful arcs. The battle was over in minutes. Actually, it was over before it even began. The British Legion had routed the Continentals.

The Hamilton brothers watched in horror as some of the men on the far right appeared to be plunging their swords and bayonets into the ground at their very feet.

"What are those men doing, James?" questioned William.

"I think they're killing the wounded. At least that's what it looks like, little brother."

Tears welled up in William's eyes. "Are they supposed to do that?" he inquired innocently.

"No, brother. They're not supposed to do that. In fact, it's just about the most horrible, cruel, cowardly thing that any man could do on a battlefield."

# CHAPTER FOUR

The boys heard a stick crack in the woods to their right.

"What was that?" hissed William.

"Something big … most likely a deer. Could be a man, though," replied James. "Stay alert."

The boys kept watch in the direction of the sound.

Moments later one of the Virginia Continentals emerged, hatless and wounded, from the thick undergrowth about fifty yards to their right. He stumbled over a tree root and slammed into a small sapling, emitting a faint, muffled cry. He collapsed to his knees.

"Come on, boys!" urged James, running toward the man.

Hearing the approaching footsteps, the wounded man rolled onto his back and immediately began to cry out, "Don't! Please! I surrender! Good God, I surrender! Please don't hurt me again! I surrender!"

"Hush, soldier!" James slapped his hand over the man's mouth. "Half of the countryside can hear all that wailing! We're not your enemies. We're Patriots out of North Carolina. You're safe. Now lie still and let me look you over."

Relief washed across the man's pale, bloody face. Blood was running from a deep gash across his forehead at the hairline. Poor William gasped when he saw all of the blood. He quickly turned his head and threw up.

"Can I please have some water?" the man begged.

"I'll get it," volunteered William, wiping his mouth with a look of shame.

James nodded at him with a soft gaze of affirmation. "It's all right, little brother. It's nothing to be ashamed of. Go fetch a couple of canteens. We need some extra water to wash him up a bit. And grab anything you can find that will work for some bandages. We have to dress his wounds."

William returned quickly with two and a half gourds of water and two linen sacks. The dehydrated man quickly downed the half-filled gourd. James took one of the other gourds and slowly poured the water over his face, gently rinsing the blood from his eyes, nose, and ears. The cleansing water revealed the tender face of a young man, probably not much older than James.

"What's your name, soldier?" asked James.

"Alexander Macon, of the Third Virginia Regiment. Just call me Alex."

"Well, Alex, I need for you to rest as best you can for a while so that we can doctor your wounds."

Alex nodded his understanding. For the next half-hour James, John, and William washed, cleaned, and bandaged his many wounds. When they were done William took off his coat and rolled it up into a pillow for the wounded soldier.

Alex smiled at William. "I want to thank you fellows. I don't know how I'll ever be able to repay you."

"It's not necessary, Alex. It's our honor and our duty. You just rest easy and drink some more water. Are you hungry?" asked James.

"Now that you mention it, I'm starved. I don't see how I could think about food at a time like this. But I think I could eat. We've been on the move so long, I haven't had a bite since last night."

"I'll fetch some ham and biscuits," volunteered William.

"And fellows, I'm so, so cold. Down to my bones. I feel a rigor coming on."

"It's all that blood you lost, I'll bet. William, grab a couple of blankets, too."

William nodded and trotted off to the wagon to grab the food and blankets.

"Alex, if you're comfortable enough, we're going to sit right here and lay low for just a little while longer and then head north along the road toward nightfall. We'll try to put as much distance as we can between us and the Legion before we make camp for the night," James explained.

"Suits me. It feels good just to lie still a bit. And it's real good to be able to see without all that blood in my eyes." He smiled at James, his spirits lifting.

"How'd you get away from down there, Alex?" inquired James. "We didn't see any more foot soldiers getting off that battlefield. Just a bunch of officers riding low and fast toward the north right after the shooting started."

"Is that a fact?" inquired Alex, eyes opening wide.

"Yes. Colonel Buford was right in the front of all of them, galloping like there was a sack full of gold at the end of the ride."

Alex looked sullen, disappointed. "I can't say as I blame them. If I'd had a horse I probably would have been running off, too. We never had a chance on that field today. The boys all knew it as soon as we saw all those dragoons lining up on us."

"So how did you get away?" James inquired again.

"I was way out on our right flank, about ten men from the end of the line. We were under orders not to fire until they were ten yards out ... which I thought was insane ... but we followed our orders. We fired one volley. I never even had a chance to reload.

"We truly thought Colonel Buford was going to surrender. After that first shot lots of the men were dropping their muskets and surrendering. I threw mine down, too, and had my hands in the air. I even caught a glimpse of a white flag over on the left, but the man carrying it went down. I assume he was hit."

"You actually saw a white flag of surrender?" asked James in disbelief.

"Yes. Definitely. But the horse soldiers still didn't stop. They rode right into us, dozens of us with hands up to surrender. The first rider that came by me was swinging his sword. He caught me right across the line of my hat. It felt like a brick had hit me. I think I passed out for just a bit."

"But how did you get off of the battlefield?"

"When I woke up I rolled over on my belly and started crawling toward some high grass to the right of our line. Whenever I heard their soldiers I lay still and played dead until I didn't hear anything else, and then started crawling again.

"I managed to make it to the tall grass and kept going. A couple of minutes later I rolled into a small creek. I washed my eyes out, made sure that I wasn't being followed, and then headed up the creek. I finally reached the woods and stumbled into you fellows."

William returned, carrying a sack of food and dragging two blankets. He helped James cover the shivering soldier.

"William, can you just pinch off some small pieces for Alex and feed them to him? Let's let him get warmed up a bit," suggested James.

William nodded and sat down near the soldier's head, and then started feeding him small morsels of the moist biscuit, with an occasional piece of salty ham.

"You're lucky you got out of there. Lots of men died," stated James.

"The blood of those Patriots is on Tarleton's hands.

He is already well known for his savagery. Now we have an actual record of it and witnesses who saw it all. I just pray that the blood of the men massacred on this field, my friends and compatriots, will not be forgotten. I'm going to make sure that people know that this was no battle today. This was a massacre in the Waxhaws!"

A single, bloody tear trickled into his ear. "I have served with some of those boys for two years, and now I'll never see any of them again."

"We'll make sure that people know what happened here today, Alex," James promised.

William, curiously quiet since the embarrassing loss of his lunch, spoke up, "You said you've served two years. Exactly how old are you, Mr. Alex?"

"I'm twenty years old, William … that's your name, isn't it?"

William nodded and smiled. He was clearly proud that Alex knew his name.

"But I feel much older than that today, William."

"You're just a year older than James!" William replied.

"I imagined that we were about the same age when I first saw your brother. So tell me, how old are you, William?"

"Oh, I'm just thirteen … way too young to be in the army."

"But not too young to fight the Legion," James interrupted. He went on to describe the events of Saturday night and how they had defeated the squad of British Legionnaires with the help of their friend Andy Jackson.

"Well, that's quite a feat, indeed! So you have seen action then, young William. I have a brother back home who is almost your age, I think. I've been gone far too long. Shadrack … we all call him Shad … must be twelve by now. I hope and pray that he will never have to fight in this war or fire his weapon at another man."

"Me, too, Mr. Alex. I decided that for myself today. I

don't ever want to shoot another man, or even shoot *at* another man, for as long as I live."

"That is an honorable decision, William. I hope, as well, that you will never again have to take up arms against another man."

"But I'm still a Patriot!" chirped William.

Alex smiled. "Of that I have absolutely no doubt. Now … can I have some more of those fine biscuits and ham?"

"My pleasure!" William carefully and tenderly fed the wounded man.

John interrupted their conversation, "It'll be pitch dark in an hour and a half, James. Do you think we ought to get on the road and get out of here?"

James replied, "Yep, let's go. Let's get Alex to the wagon."

It took several minutes to wrestle the exhausted soldier up the hill, but they finally made it. William had prepared a first-rate bed for Alex to rest upon. He took the reins and John joined him on the seat. James sat in the back, keeping watch to the south. William skillfully led the team through a shallow gully and back onto the road below the crest of the ridge, well out of sight of the battlefield.

They headed northward toward Charlotte … back toward home.

# CHAPTER FIVE

The roads did not cooperate as they had hoped. The boys struggled to make even two miles for each hour of travel. The twilight appearance of the Hamilton boys in downtown Charlotte on Tuesday afternoon with a wounded, bloody Continental soldier in their wagon caused a general disturbance. The news that a major battle had just occurred forty miles to the south threw the town into an uproar.

The boys left their wounded friend in the local doctor's good care and continued on toward home in the dark, leaving the townsfolk to their hysteria. They arrived at their cabin late in the evening. Emotionally and physically drained from their ordeal and journey, they kicked off their leggings and shoes and tumbled into their beds.

Sunrise brought a parade of visitors and curiosity-seekers, anxious for news and information about the British. Their mother and little brother, Hugh, were among the first visitors on Wednesday morning.

James, John, and William had not lived with their mother and stepfather for almost a year and a half. The boys did not get along with their stepfather, so they took the first opportunity they had to leave home and buy their own piece of land. They actually purchased their father's original farm from their stepfather. The three boys had been on their own and doing quite well with James in charge of things.

But their mother still loved them very much. She embraced her boys and wept, relieved that they had returned home safely. She brought with her two chickens and all of the fixings for a feast and insisted upon cleaning up the cabin and cooking the boys a huge "welcome home" dinner. It was exactly the homecoming that they all needed.

Folks continued to drop by for several days. The boys shared about the political situation down south, the movements of the British, and the massacre in the Waxhaws. Somehow word got out about their battle at the McClelland cabin. There was much talk about it in the community, but no one dared approach the Hamilton boys regarding their experience.

Thankfully, by week's end, life had settled back into its familiar routine of chores, farming, livestock care, and hunting.

On Friday evening after supper the boys built a small campfire on the ground near the cabin and sat down to watch the sunset. James and John puffed on their clay pipes while William played with his marbles in the smooth dirt. John soon joined in a friendly game with his little brother. It was a pleasant, peaceful, restful evening.

James broke the serenity of the moment by speaking, "Boys, I need to run up to the village of Salisbury tomorrow to do some business. I need to sell a couple of horses and a few other things so we can make a payment on our farm."

"Can I go to Salisbury with you tomorrow, James?" begged William.

"No, little brother, I'm going to go alone. It's purely a business trip. Don't worry, though. I'll be home by dark. You won't even miss me. Besides, I need you two to chop out that south cornfield tomorrow. It's getting to where I can hardly tell the weeds from the corn after all this rain we had last week."

"Oh, boy! Exciting stuff!" mocked William, rolling his eyes.

"I know doesn't measure up to the excitement you've become accustomed to lately, but it's important. Especially if you plan on eating this winter," corrected James.

"All right, all right. Chopping corn tomorrow. Got it. Can't wait," William grunted.

"Let's go ahead and call it a night, brothers. We all have a long day ahead of us tomorrow," suggested James.

John and James tapped the smoldering remnants of Virginia tobacco out of their pipes. William tossed his marbles into his doeskin bag and ran for the cabin door while the older brothers kicked dirt into the coals of the fire. They followed William inside where they all stripped down to their shirts and settled into the comfort of their corn shuck beds.

The boys slept soundly. Early the next morning James left in the pre-dawn darkness. John and William arose about an hour later. After milking and feeding the cows, feeding the chickens and collecting eggs, and checking the goats' water and feed, John fixed them a hot breakfast. He scrambled six of the morning's fresh eggs and toasted some bread in the stone fireplace oven. William was quite subdued and not his usual chatty self, obviously dreading a hot day of work in the field.

They downed their breakfast, grabbed their water jugs and tools, and headed off to the field. They chopped corn all morning, finally stopping around noon to take a little nap in the shade.

William had just dozed off when he heard a voice in the distance.

"Halloooo! Is anyone home?"

"Johnny, someone's here!" hissed William, kicking his

brother in the leg.

Both of them jumped up and ran toward the house.

The voice called out again, "Private James Hamilton!"

John and William rounded the corner of the cabin. John yelled, "James isn't here, mister. What can I do for you?"

The man spun around in his saddle, startled by the unexpected voice to his rear.

"Where is he, boy?" the man inquired.

"Gone to Salisbury on business before daybreak this morning. I expect him back by nightfall."

"I see. Are you his kin?"

"Yes, sir. I'm his brother, John. This is our other brother, William."

William tipped his hat to the man.

"Well, since ole Jamie isn't here, can I trust you to give him a message for me, son?"

"Yes, sir. Of course. What's it about?" inquired John, nosily.

"It's official business pertaining to the Regiment of the Mecklenburg County Militia, to which your brother, James, has sworn his service," the man stated. "I am Lieutenant Thomas Givins of the company commanded by my brother, Captain Samuel Givins. I bring a message regarding the call-up of the regiment."

"Oh, I see," stated John.

William frowned.

Mr. Hamilton, I would be most appreciative if you could deliver this very important message to your brother. Do you need to write it down?"

"No, sir. I'm not so good at writing, but I'll be faithful to deliver your message just like you give it to me," John promised.

"Very well, then. Please inform Private Hamilton that the Regiment is now officially on alert. Command has caught wind of a Tory uprising in the neighborhood of Lincolnton. If, indeed, the regiment is called up, riders will be dispatched with a report date. Our headquarters will be Phifer's Mill. Can you handle that message?"

"Yes, sir! The regiment is on alert, Tories are in Lincolnton, riders will instruct, muster at Phifer's Mill. Got it."

"Excellent! I bid you good day, then, John Hamilton. Perhaps I will see you at a muster one of these days soon?"

"Could be," John responded, head drooping. "But for now James says I have to stay home and take care of the farm."

"Well, I'm sure that your brother knows best. Take care, Mr. Hamilton. It was a pleasure speaking with you."

"You, too, sir."

The lieutenant clucked at his horse, spun her around, and trotted back down the road toward Charlotte.

John looked at William. Neither of them were happy.

"Does that mean James is leaving us?" William asked.

"I reckon so."

James arrived back home shortly before dark. His brothers peppered him with questions about his experience and the financial deals he had made. John informed James about the visit from Lieutenant Givins and the impending call-up of the regiment. James was not surprised. He knew that it was only a matter of time before he would have to go off to the war.

A few days later the boys went into town to buy some supplies at the general store and catch up on the news.

They were clamoring into the wagon when a voice called out from across the dusty street, "James Hamilton! Hold on there, son!"

A distinguished-looking gentleman approached from the direction of the tavern. He was dressed in a fine blue wool weskit and wore an exquisite black cocked hat.

"It's a little early in the morning for rum, isn't it, Captain?" joked James.

"I'll be the judge of that, Private. Though I haven't had a single drop today, thank you very much. I merely stopped by the tavern to spread the word regarding the regiment. I'm pleased I ran into you today. Saves me a trip out to your place. And who might these two young men be?" the gentleman inquired.

"Captain Givins, these are my brothers John and William. Boys, this is the captain of my company, Mr. Samuel Givins."

"Please to make your acquaintance, gentlemen. Your reputations precede you. I've heard all about your escapades in the Waxhaws. I salute your bravery and your patriotism." The captain bowed and tipped his hat to the boys.

"What news of the regiment, sir?" asked John curiously. "Your brother came by our place a few days ago and left me a message for James."

"Indeed," the captain replied. Turning to James he said, "Well, the time for action is upon us, I'm afraid. We will muster at Colonel Phifer's place on Friday and prepare to march. We are being assigned to a Continental command, I think. You have four days to get your affairs in order and provide for these brothers of yours."

"Yes, sir. What's the enlistment time?"

"Three months," the captain responded.

"All right. Well, I reckon we had better get on our way then, since we only have four days to prepare," James responded.

The captain extended his hand. "Excellent. I will see you bright and early on Friday then. Turn out with enough personal supplies for at least five days in the field, with all of the food that you can carry. The Continentals may provide lead and powder at some point, but there's no guarantee. Boys …" Again, the captain tipped his hat to John and William, then turned and walked toward another building down the street.

"Well, brothers, you heard him," James stated flatly. "We've got four days to get you boys set up on the farm. At least I'll be back around harvest time in September."

# CHAPTER SIX

Friday approached quickly. Throughout the week they took time after their regular chores and farm labor to plan out the next three months. James compiled a thorough list of tasks that John and William needed to perform during that time period. Though the boys knew all too well what was expected of them, it gave James some peace of mind to write everything down.

The boys also helped James prepare for his three months of duty. James organized his own clothing, electing to wear his prized pair of lace-up black leather half-boots with buckskin breeches and leggings. He planned to wear his favorite green, checkered homespun shirt, covered by his heavy off-white linen hunting frock and a thick three-inch-wide leather belt.

The brothers packed both of James' shooting bags with as much lead as they would hold. They filled his personal haversack with bundles of dried beef strips, dried beans, and dried fruit. William spent the entire day on Thursday baking sheets of hardtack. Once the rock-hard crackers cooled he carefully broke them and filled a second haversack for James. They packed a snapsack full with extra socks, a thick wool blanket, and two extra shirts.

Two full horns of powder finished out his load of supplies.

All of the work and preparation helped keep their minds off of the fact that James was leaving for a long time. The brothers had been basically on their own and inseparable for almost seven years. Though James was excited about going off and doing his duty, he still felt a pang of guilt for his brothers. And they dreaded his going.

None of them slept very well on Thursday night. James was too excited. John and William were too sad about James leaving. They dozed fitfully during the wee hours of the morning, and then finally gave up about an hour before dawn. John cooked a hot breakfast while James gathered his things. William hovered close to James, doting over his every action.

After breakfast and a trip to the outhouse, James began to strap on his supplies. John volunteered to saddle his horse.

"Saddle yours, too, little brother," James instructed. "I'll need you to go along with me. I can't take my horse on the march, so I'll need you to bring her back home from Phifer's Mill."

It didn't take John long to saddle the horses. He brought them from the barn just as James was emerging from beneath the stoop of the cabin. He had his rifle in hand and was tucking his tomahawk into his leather belt. He turned to face William.

"I know you're almost a grown man, little brother. But you need to know that John is in charge while I'm gone. I want you two to work together and take care of our home."

"I know what's expected of me, James. Don't you worry about Johnny and me. We'll be just fine. And Mama's just across the ridge. You just worry about staying alive, and getting back home in September."

James wrapped both arms around his little brother and smothered him with a huge hug. He turned and laboriously mounted his horse. William actually had to give him a little push in the rump to help him lift all of the extra weight of his food and gear. John climbed up on his horse as well. They turned and headed west in the direction of the muster ground.

John called over his shoulder, "I'll be back before dinner, William!"

William waved to them both. Once they disappeared around the bend William sighed and walked back into the empty cabin.

* * *

Life on the Hamilton farm settled back into a steady routine. James had been gone for almost a month. Managing the crops was difficult with James away, but John and William were holding their own. The oppressive heat of July had blanketed the countryside, but so far there had been abundant rains.

The corn crop was well watered, high, and healthy, as was their vegetable garden. Their hoeing days were well behind them. The shadows of the thick corn stalks now kept the weeds at bay. The boys had plenty to eat and plenty of tasks around the farm to keep them occupied.

There had been no word from James since his quick departure for Lincolnton. John learned through the rumor mill that the Mecklenburg boys had arrived too late for the battle, but it had been a great victory for the Patriot forces. There had been little news after that. Until today ...

William had taken to the woods in search of a turkey for supper. John was picking tomatoes in the garden in the early afternoon when a wagon pulled up in front of the cabin. It was Angus McHenry, an older gentleman who lived about a half-mile down the road toward Charlotte. The Scotsman's oldest son, Colin, served in the same regiment as James.

"Hallo, Johnny!" he called out in his jolly, thick Scottish tongue. "I was a hopin' that I would catch ye here at the hoose whilst I was on me way home."

"Howdy, Mr. McHenry. I haven't seen you in a while. Is everything all right?"

"Aye, aye. All is grand, laddie! I'm just on me way home from Salisbury. I went up yesterday in search of me boy, Colin. I had no trouble a findin' him. None a'tall."

"So the regiment is encamped there now?"

"Aye, Johnny. They've been sleepin' in that field ever since their first march up to Lincolnton. As soon as that battle was over the army marched 'em to Salisbury and put them into that camp. They've been a practicin' their soldierin' ever since. All manner of marchin' and drillin' and shootin' and such."

"So they're all well, then. Everyone is all right?"

"How I wish they were, laddie! There's horrible want up there. Terrible sickness and hunger! The boys have almost nothin' to eat. No provision a'tall from the Congress and, apparently, the state has nay funds, either. Our boys are scavengin' what they can from the woods and countryside, but it's a poor, pitiful sight."

John was disheartened but not surprised. Stories abounded about the lack of supplies available for the Patriot militias and the Continentals.

"What should we do?" inquired John.

"Well, son, we can do our part to help 'em all we can. I took some food to me boy yesterday and stayed the night with him in the camp. Now that I'm back home I'm a doin' all I can to spread the word regardin' their want and need. So consider yourself informed, Johnny. I know that Jamie would be most grateful for some supplies and provisions. And a visit from his brothers would be most welcome, I have nay doubt."

"Thank you, Mr. McHenry. I'll think on it and see what we can do."

"You are most welcome, Johnny. Farewell, then."

The enthusiastic Scotsman clucked at his mules and headed off in the direction of his home.

William returned from his hunting a couple of hours later with two fine turkeys tied together at the feet and hanging over his left shoulder. John greeted him near the barn.

"We had a visit earlier."

"Who was it?"

"Mr. McHenry. He just got back from Salisbury. The regiment is camped there. He says they're mighty bad off. No supplies and very little food. The army isn't providing them with anything, so they pretty much have to fend for themselves. He's spreading the word so that folks might try to help."

"That sounds like a good idea. What are we going to do?"

"I say let's load the wagon full of supplies tonight and take them to Salisbury tomorrow."

"What do you plan to take?"

"Well, we need to take as much food as we can. We have four or five hundred pounds of corn meal in the shed that's still good. We can haul almost all of that. We'll be harvesting corn soon enough, anyhow. James can share it with the other boys. Plus there's plenty of dried beef and venison.

"We can take a couple of bushels of fresh vegetables from the garden. And we can be on the lookout for deer on the way up. If we could shoot a couple of the critters along the road we could just dress them and throw them on the wagon. They should keep for a couple of hours, at least. I doubt the meat would last very long once it hit camp. It'll get cooked up quick, for sure."

"Sounds like a good plan to me. Let's get to it." William paused thoughtfully. "But to be honest, Johnny, I don't like the idea of leaving the farm unattended. I think it'll be best if one of us goes up to deliver the food and one stays here. I want to see James really badly, but it's probably best that you go and I stay put."

John nodded his agreement and smiled. "I reckon

you're right. You're getting mighty wise in your old age, little brother."

"I'm just a lot more comfortable staying put on my own place."

"All right, William. You go ahead and get those turkeys cleaned. I'll pull the wagon around and load the corn meal and dried meat. That's all we really need to do tonight. We can pick all the vegetables fresh right before I leave in the morning. I can also take a couple of jugs of fresh milk for James and his buddies."

"Boy, they'll love that for sure! As long as it doesn't go bad before you get there," William chuckled. "I'll have these turkeys cleaned up and over the fire in no time. You can take one of them for Jamie tomorrow, too!"

For the next couple of hours the boys busied themselves with their work. John loaded eight fifty-pound sacks of corn meal into the wagon. He placed them in the front of the cargo space, right behind the seat. He wanted to leave the rest of the wagon clear just in case he might be able to get a deer or two along the road. He also dug a bushel of new potatoes out of the garden and placed them in the wagon. He would wait to pick the fresh tomatoes, cucumbers, and melons in the morning. Meanwhile, William prepared the birds for supper.

They ate themselves sick on the delicious, smoky meat that night and barely ate half of one bird. Afterwards they cut up the remainder of the meat and wrapped it in clean cloth to take to James. John cleaned his rifle, packed a full shooting bag, topped off his powder horn, and then the boys went to bed early.

John was up before dawn to prepare for his journey. He went out to the barn to milk the cows. He filled two one-gallon jugs with the delicious, fatty treat. William awakened soon after sunup. After a quick breakfast they went to the garden and picked a bushel of tomatoes, a bushel of cucumbers, two bushels of squash, and six large watermelons. William stashed the leftover roasted turkey and jugs of milk under the seat beneath John's feet.

Once all of the food was loaded and covered with canvas, John hopped into the driver's seat, anxious to get on the road and maintain the freshness of the milk and vegetables.

"Keep your eyes open, Johnny," warned William. "Don't worry about me. I'll keep a good eye on things here."

"I should be back by dinner tomorrow. It'll be best if I stay tonight instead of trying to get up there and back before dark. I don't want to wear out the team."

William reached his hand up to John. "Be safe, Johnny."

"You too, William."

John snapped the reins and headed toward the northern road and the Patriot camp at Salisbury.

# CHAPTER SEVEN

John returned home the following afternoon, full of stories about his night in the camp with the men of the Mecklenburg Regiment. They were, indeed, starving and much in need when John arrived. The load of food was an incredible blessing for the men. John had even managed to shoot three deer on the way to Salisbury, providing fresh meat for a large portion of the camp.

John also told William that James and the other men of the regiment were on the move. They had left Salisbury that morning headed south in pursuit of a Tory militia force.

"Do you think they will be in any battles?" asked William.

"I don't know, William. Great big battles are usually pretty rare among the militia forces. Usually the fights with the Tory sympathizers are much smaller affairs ... ambushes and skirmishes. But I suspect that James will see some action."

"I just want him to come home. Our house is empty without him."

John smiled at his brother. "I miss him, too. But we'll be okay, won't we?"

"I hope so! As long as I can get some work out of you around here, big brother," teased William.

Of course, William was joking, because John was a very hard worker. In fact, in the coming days he began to pick up some extra work utilizing the family wagon. Most of the vehicles for hauling cargo had been confiscated by the army or local militias. Since John had a working wagon he began to receive requests from local farmers to haul their goods into Charlotte.

A couple of weeks after John's visit to Salisbury to see James, a neighbor by the name of Caleb Madison offered John a Spanish milled dollar to go into Charlotte and pick up a load of lumber for him. It was easy money, and John had the time, so he jumped at the opportunity.

John left the farm right after breakfast and headed into town. William had a full day planned out. The vegetable garden was woefully in need of attention. It had almost two weeks worth of weeds that were trying to overtake the vegetables. It would take his entire morning, but William was determined to get the job done. Besides, he liked gardening and he was easily the best gardener in the Hamilton brothers' home.

William toiled in the hot garden all morning, stopping frequently to drink plenty of water. At mid-morning he took a longer break and enjoyed some cold apple cider in the shade. The extra rest and the sugar boost from the tasty cider gave him the energy to get the job done. At noontime he placed his tools in the shed and went inside to fix some dinner and get started on the evening meal. William was quickly becoming the best cook in the cabin, as well.

He decided to make a hearty stew of chicken, potatoes, and fresh onions. William smiled as he stirred and added pepper to the pot. James absolutely loved his chicken stew. William wished that James could enjoy a bowlful for supper. He missed his big brother.

William's skin crawled when he heard a piercing voice

call from the front yard of the cabin.

"Hello in the house! Can you spare a bite for a hungry soldier?"

William trembled. Raiders and marauders were becoming more and more common on the frontier as the war progressed. It seemed that evil people were always on the lookout for opportunities to steal and inflict injury upon innocent backwoods settlers.

William grabbed his musket and cocked the hammer. Inside him a conflict erupted. He thought, "I don't want to shoot anyone, but I have to defend myself. I have to defend our home!"

William took a deep breath, cracked open the door and poked the barrel of his musket out of the crack.

William growled in his deepest possible voice, "Hold it right there, mister. One step closer and I'll blast you all the way to Charlestown."

"What's the matter with you, William? Don't you recognize your big brother's voice when you hear it?"

William flung open the door ran out into the yard, dropping his musket in the grass. He screamed, "Jamie!"

He ran to his brother with all the speed his legs could provide, tackling him to the ground and smothering him with a huge hug. James howled with joy as he clung to his little brother in the cool grass. After a few moments James extricated himself from William's grasp.

William asked expectantly, "Are you home for good?"

"No, just for one week. The whole regiment got a furlough. Where's Johnny?"

"He went into town to pick up a load of lumber for Mr. Madison. Lately folks have been paying him to haul cargo in the wagon. I keep an eye on things here are the cabin while he makes a little extra money. He should be back any time now. I've got supper warming on the hearth."

"That sounds good to me! I'm almost starved to death. What did you make?"

"I made a stew with chicken, onions, and potatoes. And a pone of cornbread is cooking right now."

"Little brother, that sounds dee-licious! John had better get on home, or I might not leave a single bite for him."

"You've got plenty of time to wash up before supper. And I don't mean to be getting into your business, Jamie … but you're a might rank. How about doing a little washing under those arms of yours?"

James smacked him in the head. "I hear you, little brother. Don't worry, I'll smell like a field of daisies when I'm done."

"I'll believe it when I smell it," William responded.

William trotted back into the house to get James some soap. He brought out a basin, a small cloth, and chunk of lye soap and then went back inside to check on his cornbread. James poured a half-bucket of water into the basin and stripped off his shirt. He was busy taking a standing bath when John pulled the wagon off the road and approached the house.

John was a bit confused at first by the sight of a man on his porch covered in mud and soap suds, but soon recognized his older brother. He brought the wagon to a halt and jumped down.

"I would hug you, but you're too much a mix of nasty and slippery right now." He beamed. "Welcome home, James."

"It's good to be home, brother."

"How long will you be here?"

"I have to be back at Salisbury in seven days. The whole regiment received furlough for a week."

"Well, that's good. It'll give us a chance to fatten you up a bit."

"That's what I'm hoping for! Supper's almost ready, according to William."

"Good, I'll take care of the horses and wash up," replied John.

By the time John finished watering and housing the horses, James had rinsed off and put on a crisp white shirt.

"You almost look human again," commented John as he walked up to the cabin.

"I almost feel human again. Maybe some hot food will finish the job. Let's eat!"

The boys went inside and, for the first time in over a month, had a family meal together. They ate the entire pot of stew and every crumb of William's cornbread. James guzzled mug after mug full of fresh milk. After dinner they took their chairs outside to watch the sunset and smoke their pipes. They talked and laughed until late into the night. James was almost too excited to go to bed, but he forced himself, anyway.

The boys rose early the next morning and got to work on the farm. James loved being back on his own place again. He loved the smell of the dirt. He loved everything about it. He was determined to savor every moment.

They worked all day Friday and Saturday. On Sunday they went to church. They sang and worshiped. Their mother wept with joy. They went to the Farr home for dinner and were invited to stay until supper. They played games with Hugh and their half-brothers and half-sisters. It was one gloriously fine and memorable day.

Mundane work on the farm continued on Monday morning. The time for the corn harvest was growing near. James would have to miss that, unfortunately. But there were still plenty of other tasks to take care of. They worked on fences until dinner, and then lay down for an afternoon nap.

James lay awake for quite some time. He was thinking too much. He was already dreading leaving. Thursday was approaching too quickly. Soon it would be time to march back to camp ... back to the hunger, want, and violence of the war. Despite his racing mind he eventually drifted off into a fitful sleep.

Something was shaking his leg. The sensation grew

stronger. Someone was trying to rouse him.

"Leave me alone!" he exclaimed.

"Someone's coming," John hissed. "I hear a horse."

James shook the cobwebs of sleep from his brain. Sure enough, he heard the high-pitched thud of a horse's hooves striking hard dirt and rock.

"It's a fast rider," stated James.

"Sounds like it," confirmed John.

The sound of the horse grew louder as it approached. James jumped from his bed. John was already holding James' rifle. He tossed it to him and then they both bolted for the door. William stood near the window with his musket at the ready. They all cocked their flintlocks. John lifted the latch and flung the rough wooden door open as James lunged out, rifle at the ready.

"Don't shoot, gentlemen!"

It was Ensign John McFalls, from James' militia company. James and John lowered their rifles, exhaling in relief.

James called over his shoulder, "Come on out, William! It's a friend!"

Ensign McFalls tipped his cocked hat to the boys. "Private Hamilton, the regiment is recalled at once. The British are out of Charlestown in force and headed north. We have been ordered to join Gates' army in South Carolina. Muster is at the Charlotte Courthouse at sunset. Bring all of the powder, lead, and food that you can carry. We will be marching hard, probably into the night and again all day tomorrow. We have many miles to travel. I'll see you there. I need you to inform your friends, Privates Moffat and Pippin. Understood?"

James replied, "Yes, sir. I'll be there. And I'll tell the boys."

The Ensign shouted, "Huzzah!" and then spun his horse and galloped to the east, headed to the next homestead.

James looked at his brother and shrugged. "Well,

brothers, I guess that's it. Cornwallis calls."

John and William didn't respond. They were already heading back inside the cabin to help organize and pack their brother's gear.

# CHAPTER EIGHT

Once again John prepared to take James to the place of muster for the regiment, this time in the wagon. James sent William on horseback to pass the word to his friends Joel Moffat and Henry Pippin.

While James was making his preparations for the deployment John packed some extra foodstuffs to take to the other soldiers. He loaded three bushels of freshly dug potatoes, two bushels of sweet corn, and two bushels of tomatoes. Since the corn crop would be in within a couple of weeks, John tossed in their last hundred pounds of corn meal.

William killed a deer about every three days, so the boys had a huge supply of dried, smoked venison. John loaded four large grain sacks full of the dried meat into the wagon as well. He figured that the men would be able to take what they wanted of the vegetables and meat to fill their haversacks.

William soon returned from his mission as messenger. Once again the older brothers left him at home and headed for the muster. William grabbed his axe, maul, and wedge and headed out to the north pasture to work on a section of broken fence. He would be splitting rails and mending fences until John returned home.

He worked steadily all morning. It wasn't bad work since most of it was in the shade. He finished one entire section of fence right before noon and broke for dinner. He rounded the corner of the cabin just as a well-known neighbor, Ned Carlisle, rode up on his mule.

"Howdy, Mr. Ned. What brings you over my way?"

"I have some bad news for you, William. Real bad. Your brother asked me to come and tell you on my way home."

William was frantic. "What? What happened? Are my brothers all right?"

"Oh, they're just fine. They just get a big surprise, that's all. Captain Givins drafted your brother, Johnny, into the wagon service for the trip down to South Carolina."

"What?" William exclaimed. "Why would he do that? John's not even in the militia, yet!"

"Well, he is now. The Captain made him raise his right hand and swear his oath of allegiance right there in front of the courthouse. The regiment needed more wagons and supplies. I guess Johnny showed up at the wrong time. He seemed all right with the notion, though. I think he was a little excited to be going."

"Well, what am I supposed to do?" asked William.

"I don't rightly know the answer to that, little man. I reckon that's up to you. James just wanted me to tell you where John was so you wouldn't be left hanging with no news or explanation. Maybe they won't be gone too long. If I were you I would sit tight and wait for them to come back home."

William hung his head. "At least Mama is close by."

"That's right. You can count on your mother, and Ephraim Far, too. I know you boys didn't get along so well with your stepfather, but he really is a good man. I know that he is there to help you if you need him."

William walked over to the skinny farmer and extended

his hand. "Thank you for letting me know about everything, Mr. Carlisle. I'll be just fine."

"All right, then. You take care of yourself, William. I'm not too far away, either. You can give me a shout if you need any help."

"Thank you, sir."

And with that, Ned Carlisle kicked the sides of his mule and urged the animal back toward the road to his home. William stood in the solitude of the clearing, wondering how long he might be alone.

He ate a lonely dinner. Afterwards he decided not to work on the fences or in the fields for the afternoon. He puttered around the barn and busied himself with several small tasks that had been overlooked for some time. He fixed a couple of shingles on the barn. He nailed a fresh board under the window of the cabin. He even repaired the rickety front porch step.

Late that afternoon he cooked some eggs for his supper, but he really wasn't very hungry. He was lonely. And to be honest, he was afraid. Despite his best efforts to appear confident and all grown up, William didn't like to be alone in the cabin at night. He was, after all, only thirteen years old. But he resolved himself to "be a man" and deal with his situation.

William didn't sleep very well that night. He imagined all sorts of strange sounds in the woods. He jumped at the sound of every hooting owl, yelping coyote, and rooting skunk or raccoon. He was relieved when the dull light of dawn began to creep through the cracks of the cabin door.

William jumped out of his bed and donned his knee-length breeches and straw cocked hat and then headed out to take care of the livestock. It had long been his responsibility to milk the huge cows, Sylvia and Barthenia. He also had to feed the chickens and gather eggs, tie the goats out in the grassy clearing, and toss slop to the pigs.

He whipped up a quick breakfast of fresh eggs, leftover cornbread, and milk. After breakfast he decided that he would take the morning off from work and go over to visit his mother. She needed to know what had happened to John. He grabbed his shooting bag and musket and headed out through the woods to the west toward his stepfather's farm.

His mother was surprised when she heard the knock at the door. She was even more surprised when she discovered the identity of her visitor.

"Willie! Oh, my boy! I am so glad to see you!"

She grabbed him in her warm arms and smothered him with kisses. She didn't get to see her sons very often after they bought their own place and left their stepfather's farm. She took advantage of every opportunity she had to shower them with the love that only a mother can provide.

She noticed the sullen look on William's face. "What's wrong, Willie? Did James or Johnny do something to you? If they've been mean to you, I swear, I'll turn them over my knee. Neither of them is too old for a sound spanking from their mum."

William chuckled at the notion of his petite mother spanking James.

"No, mama. I was just lonely."

"Lonely, pray tell why? Where's Johnny?"

"That's what I came to tell you, Mama. John's gone with James … to the war."

Margaret Farr collapsed into a chair beside the stone fireplace. She burst into tears.

"Why, William? Why would Johnny have to go? He's no soldier! He's barely sixteen years old and doesn't even serve in the militia!"

"I know, Mama. But they needed wagons and supplies. That's why they drafted him into the service. He's not actually serving as a soldier. They wanted him for a wagon driver. The army is headed into South Carolina to stop the British from coming into North Carolina. James got called up. John just went along to bring his horse back home. That's when John got drafted."

"Well, that makes some sense," answered his mother, sniffing and wiping her eyes and nose with a silk handkerchief. "Perhaps he won't be gone too long, then."

"That's what I'm hoping," answered William.

"Well, however long he's gone, you are welcome to come here as often as you like. You can stay here, if needs be. I want you to know that you can count on Ephraim and me."

William hung his head. "Ephraim won't want me in this house. He hates me. He hates all of us."

"Nonsense! He cares about you all very deeply. He just doesn't know how to show it. He's changed, Willie. In the early days he was awfully jealous of the love that I had for your father ... God rest his soul. Ephraim treated you badly because of that jealousy. But he was wrong, and he knows it now. He would love to try and make things different, if you boys will just let him."

William sighed. "It's not all up to me, but I'm willing to give him a chance."

"That's all I can ask, son. Now ... will you be staying with us tonight? I can prepare you a spot right here near the fireplace."

"No ma'am. I don't want to leave the farm at night unless I absolutely have to. I just wanted to come and visit for a while."

"And maybe enjoy a little bit of your mother's home cooking, I'll wager." She winked at her son and reached out to ruffle the hair on his forehead.

"Yes ma'am. That might help my loneliness a bit." He smiled sheepishly.

"Well then, how's about you go out to the rooster pen and bring me in a couple of birds? There are two of those big red monsters that have been causing all manner of trouble among the hens. We penned them up with the other roosters, but all they want to do is fight. It's high time they found some flour and a hot skillet. Do you think you can capture the beasts?"

"Oh, yes ma'am!" William's mouth watered at the thought of hot fried chicken.

"Well, be on your way, then. It'll be dinner time before we know it."

William caught and butchered the two unruly roosters and brought the fresh meat in for his mother. One hour later he was seated at the table with his "other" family … all of his half siblings. It was a house full of little Farrs, actually. He stole a glance at his stepfather right after the blessing. Ephraim Farr nodded and winked at William, offering a soft smile of welcome.

William was very glad that he had decided to visit that day. It lifted his spirits tremendously. But he knew he still had work to do on his own farm, so he bid farewell shortly after the noon meal and trudged through the woods back to his cabin home.

He worked at various tasks throughout the afternoon and was just preparing to go inside and begin work on his evening meal when he heard the familiar rattle of the family wagon coming up the road. Johnny was back home!

# CHAPTER NINE

William exploded, "What? James has been captured?"

John nodded. "Yep. The whole regiment was captured. Gates' entire army was either killed or captured. It was a rout. The battle happened at a place called Camden."

"So what happens now?" asked William.

"I don't know. I guess we wait and hope that he'll be released or exchanged soon. I reckon the first thing we need to do is pray that he was actually captured."

William knew what that meant. Johnny didn't know for sure that James had been captured. He might have died in the battle. There was no way to know.

\* \* \*

A full month passed after James' disappearance at Camden. For John and William it was the not knowing that was so hard. Not knowing if James was dead or alive. And if by some miracle he was alive, not knowing where he was being held, or if he was wounded, sick, or had enough food to eat. Not knowing was what kept the boys awake at night.

So to combat their despair the Hamilton brothers stayed busy on the farm. Work was one of the few mechanisms at their disposal to help alleviate the absence of James. Yet at the same time his absence was such a huge burden on their work. For years James had been the true leader and workhorse on their small farm. He was the foreman and his brothers were the laborers. It had always been that way and it had always worked very well.

But somehow John and William managed. The corn crop came in around the first of September. It was a bumper crop. They managed to bring in the harvest with a little help from Ephraim Farr and his hired workmen. John traded the bulk of the corn to the mill in exchange for ground corn meal and flour for winter storage. The boys fully stocked their own corncrib and even built a second crib to store ear corn for the livestock throughout the winter.

The vegetable garden was still producing into early September. William worked the garden like a master. He had a real talent for it. He put in the cold-weather crops at the end of August. They would have ample turnips to add to the potatoes, onions, carrots, and beets in the root cellar. There would also be plenty of tasty cabbage for the fall.

William spent quite a bit of time at their mother's place. He ate often at his mother's table. He played with the other kids. He even spent some nights at the Farr home, something that he would have never done if James were at home.

John, on the other hand, had other priorities. He had courting on his mind. He began to spend lots of time at the John Skillington homestead. Each week he spent Friday and Saturday evenings and Sunday afternoons with the oldest daughter in the home, Mary Skillington. John and Mary were helplessly, hopelessly in love with one another. William imagined that his brother would marry the young woman in another year or two.

Amazingly, despite the proximity of recent battles and the loss of over two hundred men from the local area at the Battle of Camden, the war had still not encroached upon the actual borders of the county of Mecklenburg. There were still skirmishes and engagements ongoing down in South Carolina, and the Tories to the north and east seemed emboldened by the British victories.

Cornwallis, however, had stopped his army in the Waxhaws in South Carolina after his huge victory at Camden. The reason for his pause was unknown, but it was most welcome. And so the people of Charlotte and the surrounding areas had enjoyed an entire month of peaceful respite.

But all of that changed in late September of 1780.

John was enjoying a leisurely afternoon at the Skillington farm when his stepfather, Ephraim Farr, rode up on his horse. John walked out to meet him.

"What's wrong, sir? Did something happen to William?"

"No, John. I'm just here to deliver a message. Patriot spies have gotten word through that the British are preparing to move north. The report is that they will pull out of the Waxhaws and head north in the next few days. General Davidson has called up all the area militiamen who can and will serve and is asking every able-bodied man to report for duty at the courthouse at dawn day after tomorrow. I promised to bring the message out this way."

"All right. Thank you, sir. I will be there. Is there anything else?"

"No, son. I'll see you Tuesday at dawn. And I'll make sure William just stays at our house with your mother until this all blows over."

"Thank you, sir. That really does help set my mind at ease."

"I knew it would." He smiled at John ... a sincere, caring smile. It seemed strange to John, but not unpleasant. "Bring lots of food and lead. I'll have a horn of powder for you."

Ephraim turned his horse and rode back toward his home. Mary came quickly from the house, her parents right behind her.

"What is it, Johnny? What's wrong? Is somebody hurt?"

"No, Mary. No one is hurt. It was about the militia. Ephraim was just delivering a message."

"What message?" inquired John Skillington, walking up to the young couple.

"It's about the British, sir. General Davidson has gotten word that the Redcoats are pulling out of the Waxhaws and heading north. They expect them to be here some time Tuesday or after. The militia's been called up. All able-bodied men who will serve are expected at the courthouse at dawn day after tomorrow."

"So you're going?" inquired Mrs. Skillington.

"Yes, ma'am. I'm a sworn member of the regiment."

"I guess I'll see you Tuesday morning, then," remarked John Skillington.

John nodded his response. He turned to Mary. "I have to go home now and get ready, Mary. I'll come and see you when this is all over."

Mary smiled. "Prepare well, and take care of yourself, Johnny Hamilton. I have plans for you."

Tuesday, September 26, came quickly. Ephraim Farr and John Skillington arrived at the Hamilton boys' cabin shortly before sunrise. John had just finished his breakfast and gathered his supplies. He walked out of the front door with his rifle in his hand.

John stopped and turned to his little brother. "I'll be back as soon as this is all over."

William hugged his brother. "You just be careful, Johnny. I need you around here."

"I'll be careful. I promise."

Ephraim Farr spoke, "William, I want you to gather

your things and go to my house and be with your mother. I don't like leaving her alone with the kids. If something happens to me, I need a man at the house to help her."

William nodded at his stepfather. "Yes, sir. You can depend on me."

John Hamilton, John Skillington, and Ephraim Farr turned and rode their horses silently along the road headed southwest toward Charlotte just as the dull light of dawn filtered into the eastern sky. They were going to fight the Redcoats.

William stood and watched them riding away, wondering if he would ever see either of his brothers again.

He finished his chores in the cabin and barn and then prepared to go to the Farr homestead. He prepared for a stay of several days, packing a large snapsack full of extra socks, shirts, and supplies. He grabbed his musket and set out on foot through the woods on the familiar trail to his mother's house.

The typical yard full of Farr children greeted him upon his arrival, as well as his baby brother, Hugh. Hugh was the youngest son of his father, the late Hugh Hamilton. Hugh was a baby, less than two years old, when his father died from a tragic fall off of a friend's barn. Ephraim had treated the baby a little more kindly in those early days of his marriage to Hugh Hamilton's widow and had, in time, accepted him as his own son.

William enjoyed spending time with the ten-year-old Hugh. Though a few years younger than William, they had a lot in common and they played well together. Hugh enjoyed following William around and imitating the actions of his big brother. William actually enjoyed being the big brother for a change.

The kids had a fun-filled morning and enjoyed a big family picnic dinner under the shade at noontime. Margaret Hamilton was a wonderful mother and took great joy in seeing all of her youngest children at play in the pasture beside her home. It was a peaceful, serene scene.

But that peace was shattered when Ephraim Farr came galloping fast along a deer trail to the west. He skidded to a stop in front of the barn and jumped off of the exhausted, foaming horse. Hugh took the reins and pulled the horse toward the trough in the shade of the barn.

His wife exclaimed, "Ephraim! What on earth is wrong? Why did you torture that poor horse to the point of frothing at the mouth?"

Ephraim emptied a canteen of water over his own head in an attempt to cool his scorched red skin. He was breathing heavily. He finally got his breath.

"The British have taken Charlotte! Tarleton's dragoons overwhelmed our defenses. The Redcoats are everywhere."

"Where's Johnny?" she demanded.

"He's been taken to John Skillington's cabin."

"What do you mean, 'taken?'"

Ephraim placed both hands on his wife's shoulders and looked her square in the eye.

"Sweetheart, John Skillington pulled him off of the defense line and managed to get him onto his horse. They rode out of Charlotte when I did. John's hurt really badly. He's wounded in his head."

Margaret Farr's eyes rolled back in her head and she fainted, falling limply onto the loose, red dirt.

William grabbed his musket and took off running toward the Skillington farm.

Ephraim called out, "William, wait!"

William ignored him and kept running.

# CHAPTER TEN

William reached the farm almost a half-hour later. It wasn't very far to the Skillington place, but he had to cross some rough country. William burst through the front door. He was shocked by what he found.

John was stripped to the waist and lying on a bed in the corner. The bed was covered in blood. Mary and Mrs. Skillington were working feverishly to clean and bandage his wounds.

"What happened? Is he shot?" demanded William.

John Skillington walked to him, placing a hand on his shoulder. "No, son, John didn't get shot. He had a large stone from a wall fall and hit him across the back of the head. It cut him wide open and he's swelled up pretty bad."

"How did a stone fall on him?"

"John shot the horse out from under one of those British Legion men. The horse kept running right into the wall in front of John. It knocked the rocks loose, I reckon. He's got another cut beside his eye. I think the horse's teeth actually did that."

"Is he going to be all right?"

"I think so. He's lost a lot of blood. But he's

breathing just fine."

"Has he been awake at all?"

"No, William. That rock knocked him out cold when it hit him. He's been out ever since."

Tears formed in William's eyes. He blurted out, "First Jamie, and now Johnny, too! What am I going to do?"

"I'll tell you what you're going to do … you're going to be strong and not lose hope. You're going to be a man and take care of your farm and hold things together for your brothers. Do you think you can do that?"

William nodded, "I can do that."

"Good. Now I need you to get on out of here. I don't think I was followed when I left town, but I can't be sure. I don't want you to get caught with a musket in your hand if a detail of Redcoats shows up. Go back to your Mama's place and tell her to get on over here. We could use her help taking care of John."

"Yes, sir. I'll go fetch her right now."

"Good. Now get going."

William turned and took off running for the Farr farm, retracing his steps along the path that he had blazed just minutes before.

\* \* \*

Life flowed into a steady rhythm for William at the Farr homestead. Each morning Hugh accompanied him back to his own farm to take care of the livestock and milk the cows. It was hard work and a lot of travel. And it wasn't easy getting the milk back to the Farr cabin, but William and Hugh eventually worked out a system. The hard work helped distract William from the chaos that surrounded him.

General Lord Cornwallis of the British army had set up his headquarters in Charlotte. His officers had pretty much taken over every other house and building in and around town for their quarters. His army camped just south of town along the road. Once he was settled and in firm control of the town, Cornwallis started issuing proclamations and lording over the local people.

One of his very first actions was an attempt to disarm the citizens. The day after he took the town he issued a decree to all of the folk of Charlotte and Mecklenburg County that they were to give up their firearms and stay peacefully in their homes. He declared that the local people were now under the protection and jurisdiction of the King's army.

Next he went after food and supplies. He began to confiscate everything that he could find in order to feed his two thousand soldiers. The British took almost 30,000 pounds of flour and grain from Polk's mill, the primary mill in the area, within the first two days. They slaughtered one hundred head of cattle each day to keep the army supplied in meat. The cattle population was dwindling fast.

Of course, Cornwallis promised everyone British money for all the goods, but no one received any payment. Most of the local farmers began hiding their food and supplies ... even their cattle and sheep ... deep in the woods. One particularly enthusiastic Patriot burned his barn to keep the British from getting his grain.

William knew full well that his family's entire supply of corn and all of the flour that they traded for had been housed at Polk's mill. Their entire crop was gone. It would be a long, hungry winter.

John woke up on the second day after the battle for Charlotte. By Sunday he felt well enough to move about. He attended church with the Skillington family. They attended the Poplar Tent Presbyterian Church, the same church that the Hamiltons and Farrs had attended since they arrived in North Carolina.

William saw his brother riding up to the church in the Skillington wagon. He ran out to meet him. He'd heard that his brother was doing fine, but he had not seen him since he awakened from his state of unconsciousness.

William exclaimed, "Brother, it is good you see you!"

"I'm glad to see you too, squirt," quipped John, grabbing his younger brother in a bear hug.

"I hear you broke a stone wall with your head," joked William.

John laughed out loud, and then reached up to grab his throbbing head. "Don't make me laugh, Willie. It hurts too bad!"

"Let's go inside," encouraged William.

So the boys went to church together. Afterwards the Farrs invited the Skillingtons and John over for a picnic and family time, and they gratefully accepted. Everyone had a marvelous time eating, telling stories, and laughing. The children played merrily in the meadow below the house. It was a perfect Sunday afternoon.

Mrs. Skillington brought an end to the time of rest and leisure. "John, dear, it's time to be heading home, don't you think? Cows will need milking soon."

"Yes, my love, it is about that time." He extended his hand to his host. "Ephraim, we are grateful for your hospitality. We have truly enjoyed this afternoon of rest. Maybe we can treat you folks next Sunday."

"That sounds good to me, John. We'll plan on it."

John Hamilton spoke up, "Mr. Skillington, I would sure like to take a look at my place before heading back to your cabin. William and Hugh will be going over to milk our cows here in a bit. Would you be all right with the notion of Mary riding with me and paying the place a visit? We won't be long, I promise."

John Skillington pondered for a moment. "I reckon it'll be all right, John. Just make sure you boys are all armed, and don't take any chances. Cut cross-country and stay off the road."

"Yes, sir. I was thinking exactly the same thing."

"And make sure you're both back well before dark. If I have to come looking for you you're liable to get another knot on your skull."

"Yes, sir." John smiled.

A few minutes later three horses were headed east through the thick woods to make the quarter-mile journey to the Hamilton farm. William and Hugh had an odd assortment of empty jars and jugs tied across the necks of their horses for carrying Sylvia and Barthenia's rich milk back to the Farr cabin. Mary rode behind John, her arms locked tightly around his waist. It was a perfect afternoon for a ride. The air was cool and pleasant. John was excited to be able to visit his home.

William, who was leading the small column, brought his horse to a rather sudden stop.

"Do you smell that?" he asked.

John took a deep breath. He smelled smoke. "Smells like a campfire."

"Something's not right, Johnny," William stated urgently. "I think I see black smoke up ahead."

A sudden fear gripped them both. They were very close to their cabin … their home.

"The cabin!" William exclaimed. He screamed at his horse, "Hyah!" He dug his feet into her sides and galloped off toward the cabin as quickly as the mare would run.

His heart almost ripped in two at the sight that awaited him when he emerged from the trees. Their beloved cabin and barn, built by their father's own hands, were both engulfed in flames.

Hugh pointed to a fencepost next to the burning barn. "What's that?"

There was a large piece of paper nailed to the post. John ran over and grabbed the paper. Mary leaned over his shoulder to read what it said. She gasped, covering her mouth with her hand.

William exclaimed, "What does it say, John?"

John trembled as he read it out loud, *"REWARD. Ten Guineas Gold for the Capture or Bodies of the Traitors and Outlaws James Hamilton & William Hamilton & John Hamilton.*

*Wanted for the Murder of His Majesty's Brave and Faithful Soldiers. By Order of His Excellency General Lord Cornwallis."*

# CHAPTER ELEVEN

"This is because of what happened on the McClelland farm, isn't it?" asked William.

John nodded. "There aren't many Tories around here, but it only took one to tell about our fight on the McClelland farm. It's enough that we fought and killed five of the British Legion soldiers. But I'm sure that the story has gotten even wilder and more far-fetched every time that it's been told. There's no telling what we've been accused of."

William looked woefully at the house and barn. "Well, at least they didn't get all of our livestock. Hugh and I hid them deep in the woods earlier this week."

"Good thinking, little brother." He sighed. "Well, there's no use sticking around here and watching it burn. We'll rebuild our cabin someday ... when this horrible war is over."

"Yes we will!" stated William, determined.

The British had declared war on the Hamilton family, so John and William decided to declare war right back on them. The day after the British burned their home they made contact with Captain James Thompson of the Mecklenburg militia. They stated their desire to join the growing guerilla force that was harassing Cornwallis.

The captain welcomed them and added John to the contact list for future action against the enemy. Now all they had to do was wait for a call-up. Captain Thompson informed them that they were free to harass the British as they saw fit, but they did so at their own risk.

"But to tell the truth, we could use William for a mission right now," stated the captain.

"What kind of mission?" inquired William.

"We need information. We can't get any men into town to obtain intelligence on the enemy. It's too risky. But William could get right into their headquarters and not even be noticed."

John interrupted, "Captain, you're asking William to be a spy. They could hang him if he gets caught."

The captain nodded, "Yes, that could happen. But honestly, John, William already has a price on his head. The Redcoats could hang him anyway, if they caught him and if that's what they wanted to do."

John nodded his agreement. "He'll have to have some sort of disguise. We don't want anyone to recognize him and tell the Redcoats who he is."

"I've already thought of that," stated the captain. "We would like to send him in as a Tory messenger from Charlestown."

"What?" exclaimed John. "How could he pretend to be that?"

"Well, we captured one of their uniformed messengers about ten miles south of town yesterday. He's a young lad, not much older than William and about the same size. He carried a marked case of dispatches for Lord Cornwallis. We can take William south of the village and send him in disguised as that messenger. But it must be done today."

"Why can't I be the messenger?" asked John.

"Because you're a foot taller and fifty pounds heavier than skinny little William," remarked the captain. "He's the only Patriot that I know of who can pull this off."

William interrupted their banter, "I'll do it."

John spoke out, "But, William …"

"I said I'll do it!" interrupted William. "You two have been talking about me as if I weren't even here. Johnny, this isn't up to you. It's my decision. This is my chance to serve the cause. I'll do it!"

The captain nodded his approval. "Very well, then. William, let's turn you into a Tory messenger!"

* * *

William hated the uniform that he was wearing. It was made of rough, itchy wool. But the worst part was that it was red. He wore the trademark red and blue coat of the South Carolina Royalist Regiment. And then there was the silly wig that the captain made him wear. He tugged at the dark curls. It was humiliating.

William was waiting in the woods one mile south of Charlotte, ready to begin his gallop into town. He just hoped that none of the Mecklenburg County guerillas took a shot at him along the road. The captain had promised him that it wouldn't happen. To help convince the British of his identity, the Patriots set up a fake ambush a half-mile south of Charlotte. Twelve men were assigned to fire their muskets and rifles into the air as William rode by.

John and Captain Thompson sat on horseback beside William.

"All right, William, you're solid on our plan, aren't you?"

"Yes, sir. I gallop past the fake ambush as fast as I can, and then as soon as the town comes into view, I turn and fire my pistol down the road."

"Exactly! And if our little ruse works, you should be able to walk right into Cornwallis' office. Try to get any information that you can. Find out about troop movements. We particularly need to know what their next target might be. If we can figure out where they're taking a large column of troops, we can set up an ambush and do some significant damage."

"Yes, sir. I'll try to find out what I can. What if they ask a lot of questions or make me stay in town?"

The captain cautioned, "Try to tell as few lies as possible ... they get harder to remember the more of them you tell. Keep your answers vague. Don't claim to know anyone you don't really know. They will, most likely, give you dispatches to take back to Charlestown tomorrow. Just ride south like a normal messenger. We'll be right here on this spot waiting for you."

"Yes, sir." William took a deep breath. "I think I'm as ready as I'll ever be."

"All right, then. Good luck and God speed." The captain shook his hand. "You're a brave Patriot, William Hamilton."

John stared at his little brother. "You be careful, little brother. I don't want to have to explain to Mama how I went and let you get your neck stretched."

"I'll be fine, Johnny. I'll see you at supper tomorrow."

William clucked at his borrowed horse and began to head north toward Charlotte, gradually increasing his speed. A half-mile north a group of men mingling along the road waved at him as he approached. William waved back. The men ducked into the woods. Just as William reached their position they unleashed a ragged volley of shots into the air and screamed a chorus of war whoops.

William kicked his horse and snapped the reins. He leaned forward over its neck and held on tightly as the horse reached an all-out gallop. He could hear the thunder of his horse's hooves. It was actually a magnificent animal. It ran like the wind. Moments later Charlotte came into view. William could see a cluster of soldiers gathering in the center of the road.

"This is it!" William thought.

He pulled his English flintlock pistol from his belt, cocked the hammer, and spun sideways, firing a single shot down the empty road.

The Redcoats in the roadway rapidly formed a line, their muskets at the ready.

"Oh, Lord, please don't let them shoot me!"

Just as William approached the line of soldiers, the ones in the middle moved aside and gave him an opening through which he might pass. He galloped through the gap and then looked back over his shoulder to see the Redcoats close ranks behind him. The line of twelve soldiers then fired a concentrated volley at their imaginary enemy.

The ruse had worked! William was in Charlotte, and they believed him to be a Loyalist soldier!

# CHAPTER TWELVE

An officer standing near one of the larger homes in town, formerly Colonel Polk's house, waved at William to flag him down. William pulled his horse to a stop in front of the home. He looked around and acted like he had never seen the village before.

"State your business, Private!" barked the officer with a heavy English accent.

"Sir, I'm Private William Harper of the South Carolina Royalist Regiment, bearing dispatches from Charlestown for General Cornwallis." William patted the pouch under his arm.

"We expected you yesterday, son. Why the delay?"

William expected this challenge. He replied, "My horse went lame just north of Camden. It took some time to find me a replacement mount."

The officer seemed satisfied with his explanation. "Very well, give me your dispatches and await further instructions at the tavern."

"Begging your pardon, sir, but I don't know you. These dispatches are for General Cornwallis. I must insist that I hand them over to him personally."

The officer smiled. "Good answer, private. You have

been trained well. Follow me and I will make your introduction." He turned to a Redcoat soldier standing nearby. "Corporal, see to this man's horse. See that it is watered, fed, and prepared for a return to Charlestown in the morning."

"Yes, sir!" the corporal responded.

William climbed down from the tall horse and handed the reins to the soldier.

The officer raised one eyebrow. "Goodness, aren't you a tiny little fellow? How did you ever get into His Majesty's service? How old are you, boy?"

"Fifteen sir. My father volunteered me for messenger service. They needed men who were small and light and who knew how to ride."

"I see. Well, you certainly fit the bill, don't you?" The officer smiled at him, revealing several woefully crooked teeth.

William smiled back. "That's why I'm here and not back home in Charlestown, sir."

"Quite. Come along, then." The officer led William through the gate into the yard and up the steps into Colonel Polk's house. William followed the man to a set of closed double doors. It was the entrance to the study that served as General Cornwallis' office.

The officer cautioned, "I will introduce you to the general. Do not speak unless you are spoken to. Answer only the questions that the general asks. Do you understand?"

"Yes, sir."

"Excellent." The officer swung open both doors.

"Lord, a messenger has arrived bearing dispatches from Charlestown. He insists upon delivering those dispatches personally. The boy experienced difficulties with his horse near Camden. A replacement animal had to be obtained, causing a delay."

The general was seated in the huge leather-bound chair behind the desk. He looked over the top of his reading glasses and evaluated William.

After a few moments he looked back down at his papers and then spoke, "Did you encounter any difficulty on the highway?"

William cleared his throat. "Not until I arrived here, sir. I was ambushed about a mile outside of town."

The general glanced up at him. "I see that you escaped unscathed."

"Yes, sir. I was riding pretty fast. I don't think they were expecting me."

The general grunted. "Your were lucky, indeed. I've lost at least a dozen messengers in the past week alone. This is an agreeable enough village, but it is a veritable hornet's nest of rebellion. The people of this county are more hostile to England than any other place in America."

William remained solemn and standing at attention, but he smiled on the inside.

The general ignored him as he studied the maps and papers in front of him.

"Major Edwards, come here for a moment."

The major answered, "Yes, sir!" He scurried to the general's desk.

"Major, one of our operatives has indicated that there is a treasure trove of supplies at the farm of a man named McIntyre located here, approximately eight miles north of the village." The general pointed to a spot on his map. "Have we reconnoitered that location yet?"

The major examined the map. "No, General. There have been rumors of supplies at that farm, but I have not risked sending a detail due to its considerable distance from our forces here in Charlotte."

The general waved his hand dismissively. "We cannot tarry any longer. The needs of our army outweigh the risks. I want you to take a detail in force to that location tomorrow morning at first light. Assign at least four hundred infantry and dragoons. Take every available wagon. We should have at least fifty at our disposal by now. Put on a show of force. The rebels won't dare attack such an imposing enemy."

"Yes, sir. I will make arrangements forthwith."

William's mind was reeling. This was exactly the information that he was trying to obtain! He knew when the British were moving out, where they were headed, and how many of them there would be! He had to get this information to the militia tonight! William suddenly felt a rush of excitement and anticipation.

"Being a spy is exciting!" thought William.

The general realized that the messenger was still standing at attention before him. He took off his glasses and leaned back in his chair.

He spoke to William, "Young man, you are to be commended for your bravery and your ability to deliver your correspondence. Please leave my dispatches with the major. He will arrange a meal and a room for you. I doubt that I will have any messages prepared tomorrow, so you may spend the day at your leisure. However, I expect you to be prepared to return to Charlestown the day after tomorrow."

William snapped his heels and stood up straight and tall, "Yes, sir! And thank you sir!"

The general put his glasses back on and looked down at his map. "You are dismissed."

"Yes, sir!"

William spun around and headed out the door, following the major. Once outside he handed the leather case to the officer. The major walked over to his desk in the corner and scratched out a note on a small piece of paper.

"Private, this is a voucher for a hot meal today and tomorrow and a bed for two nights. Take it to the tavern down the block. They have a small room that we have kept available for messengers. They will attend to your needs."

"Thank you, sir," William responded.

"Report back to me for your orders at daybreak day after tomorrow."

"Of course, sir."

"You are dismissed. Get some rest. Good show, by the way, getting past those marauders on the highway. You showed skill and cunning. You made quite an impression on Lord Cornwallis. I'd say he has taken quite a liking to you."

William smiled at the officer. He lied brazenly, "The feeling is mutual, sir."

He turned and walked out the door, placing his black British cocked hat on his head as he walked down the steps.

William thought proudly, "So … General Cornwallis thinks Charlotte is a 'hornet's nest' of Patriots. I'll show him! I'm the toughest little hornet in town! I'm going to make sure his column of wagons gets blasted back to South Carolina!"

William made his way to the tavern and secured his room. He wanted to remain out of sight as much as possible, just in case someone in town might recognize him. He asked the attendant to bring his meal upstairs to him so that he could eat in private. The food arrived about an hour later. He devoured the plate of food and then settled in to wait for darkness.

Throughout the afternoon William noted the movements of the sentries. He watched their patterns and the directions that they took as they patrolled. He soon discovered an opening in their perimeter not far from the tavern. He decided that he would wait until midnight, when everyone but the sentries was asleep, to make his break for the woods.

He had no choice … he had to get word to the militia about the British mission planned for tomorrow morning!

William was nervous. He paced all around the room, wishing that the sun would go down. At long last midnight arrived. He hadn't seen a sentry in quite some time.

He thought, "Now is the time to get away!"

He quietly opened a window in his room that faced the woods to the rear of the tavern. Quietly, stealthily, he crawled through the window and hung from the sill by his fingertips. He counted to three and then let go, dropping noisily to the rocky ground below. He crouched down low and glanced around to see if anyone was watching. Seeing no one he eased into the woods and soon found a deer path to follow to the north.

He moved steadily and quietly away from town, stopping only once to turn his red British coat inside out. He didn't want a local bushwhacker to think he was actually a British soldier and shoot him. Almost two hours later he arrived at the Farr cabin. He walked up to the door and tapped quietly.

A voice growled from inside, "Don't move a single step, or I'll blast you through this door!"

"Ephraim! Johnny! It's me! William!"

Ephraim Farr flung open the door. John stepped onto the porch in his nightshirt and stared at his little brother in disbelief.

John peppered him with questions. "How did you get out of Charlotte? Why are you here? Why did you leave so soon?"

William interrupted him, "I already found out what we need to know, Johnny! The British are moving on McIntyre's farm first thing in the morning. Over four hundred men and fifty wagons." He paused. "Not bad for a brand new spy, huh?"

John smiled, revealing his gleaming white teeth in the darkness.

"Not bad at all, little brother. Let's saddle our horses. We've got to go tell Captain Thompson right now!"

# CHAPTER THIRTEEN

Captain Thompson was thrilled about the information that William had obtained on his spy mission. He immediately sent runners to inform all of the local militia and call them to action. John Hamilton was one of those runners. He took off on his horse to inform the men to the east of Charlotte.

The captain looked at William. "Son, you look exhausted."

"Yes, sir. I'm tired, for sure. I don't usually stay up into the middle of the night."

"Well, you've done your part. You obtained the intelligence that we need to inflict some real damage on Cornwallis and his army. Go on home and get some rest. It'll be sunup in a couple of hours. We'll let you know how things turn out."

"Thank you, sir. I believe I'll do just that. I don't think I can stay awake a minute longer."

The captain patted William on the shoulder. "Good work, lad. You've served your country very well on this night."

"Thank you, sir. It was an honor."

"And it's an honor to have you serving under my

command. Now go on home."

"Yes, sir."

William left the cabin and climbed exhausted up onto his horse. A half hour later he was sound asleep in his bed, still wearing his boots and the captured British clothes.

\* \* \*

Later that morning the Patriot militia sprung its trap. A group of farmers attacked the British as they raided the McIntyre farm and stole the family's livestock and food stores. Thinking that they were under attack by a large force, the column of British wagons raced back toward Charlotte.

The militiamen sprung part two of their trap along the road. They managed to stop the first wagon in the British column along a narrow stretch of the highway and caused a tremendous collision, completely blocking the road. The British soldiers were "sitting ducks."

Sharpshooters from the Mecklenburg Regiment attacked the fleeing British from the location of the "traffic jam" all the way back to Charlotte. The Redcoats were under continuous attack over an eight-mile stretch of road. They suffered tremendous losses.

The frustrated, decimated convoy of British wagons finally completed the trek back to Charlotte. The drivers ran the wagon teams so hard that several of the horses fell dead in the streets of the town. They were still tied to the tongues of their wagons. Dead Redcoats littered the road all over the eight-mile stretch to the McIntyre farm. Dozens more were wounded. It was a humiliating defeat, indeed.

Cornwallis' frustrations reached their breaking point. It was inexcusable that over four hundred of his best soldiers had been humiliated by a gaggle of farmers. The General stood on the deck at the top of the courthouse steps and surveyed the mess in the streets before him.

He turned to his officers and declared, "Like I have said before, this village is a hornet's nest of rebellion. These people hate England!"

The Patriots of Mecklenburg County kept constant pressure on the occupying British. The terrain was very much in their favor. The roads of the county were narrow and surrounded by thick woods. The local sharpshooters continued their regular attacks on the British as they maneuvered along the roadways.

Though they did not inflict significant losses upon the enemy, their constant, stinging attacks did much to hamper their foraging efforts. The British radius of influence shrunk smaller and smaller, and their area of control began to dwindle. The hornets of Mecklenburg County were most definitely "out of the nest."

Cornwallis' army was beginning to run low on supplies. His men were getting hungry, and he was not happy. His couriers were being ambushed at every turn, making it impossible for Cornwallis and his officers to procure any useful military intelligence. Even the experienced and tested soldiers under his command were ready to return to the relative safety and peace of South Carolina.

The final blow to the British plan to occupy North Carolina came in the form of a message early in the morning on October 10. A lone British messenger brought almost unbelievable news to Cornwallis. A ragtag army of North Carolina and Virginia mountain men had wiped out the command of Major Patrick Ferguson, the protector of Cornwallis' western flank, three days prior at a place called King's Mountain.

Cornwallis' invasion of North Carolina was doomed.

On the afternoon of Thursday, October 12, 1780, the British Army began its evacuation of Charlotte. A pouring rain and persistent harsh wind began just as the entourage of over two thousand soldiers, another two thousand Tories and civilian camp followers, and dozens of wagons made their way southward toward Camden.

In their haste the force abandoned twenty wagons full of equipment that included tents, uniforms, and muskets. They also left behind dozens of their dead soldiers, all buried in shallow graves in the yard of a makeshift hospital at Liberty Hall School.

In just fifteen days Cornwallis' first invasion of North Carolina ended in dismal failure. The occupation was over. Mecklenburg County was, once again, free.

\* \* \*

With the threat of confiscation and outright theft gone, William and John elected to relocate all of their livestock to the Farr farm for safety and ease of care. They wholeheartedly joined in the work of their stepfather's farm. They had no other choice, really. Their home had been destroyed and the British army had already stolen and consumed their entire crop of grain.

They were dependent upon the good graces of Ephraim Farr, but they were also determined to earn their keep. When not performing the everyday chores involved in running the farm, the boys joined Ephraim in his salt-mining operation. His product was much in demand with the Continental Army.

Farm work began to dwindle dramatically as the autumn ceded its daylight and warmer air to the shorter, colder days of winter. The boys turned to hunting and tanning hides to occupy their extra time in the cooler weather. With the help of their mother they built a small, but profitable, cottage industry that produced deerskin leggings for sale and trade to the Continental Army soldiers now encamped near Charlotte.

The sprits of the people around Charlotte were lifting. The people did not have much food or money. They were barely getting by, hunting to put meat on the table and searching the woods for anything that was edible.

But at least they were free from British oppression. The direction of the war was changing. The people could sense it. The upstart little country known as the United States of America was going to win!

William and John were healthy and happy, surrounded by friends and loved ones. But they never stopped wondering about their big brother, James. Was he still alive? Would they ever see him again?

# CHAPTER FOURTEEN

Christmas was shaping up to be a joyous time for John and William. There would be little in the way of gifts, but the time among family and friends was sure to be sweet, indeed. Christmas Eve was on Sunday. The church leaders already had plans to forego regular morning services that day and, instead, have a candlelight service at sundown. These yearly Christmas Eve services at the Poplar Tent Presbyterian Church always drew a large crowd. William looked forward to it immensely.

The candlelight service was beautiful, indeed. Each of the participants brought their own candle from home. They lit the candles, bathing the tent in their soft glow, and they sang hymns. The people shared openly about the trials of the past year and the blessings that they enjoyed now that the British were gone. The congregation responded with hearty "Amens" and "Hallelujahs."

It was a heartwarming gathering. Elder William Scott, the leader of the church, finally read the story of the Nativity from the Scriptures, the typical ending to the service. The church people began to gather their belongings and await the closing prayer.

The Elder spoke to the crowd, "Friends, before we

dismiss in prayer and return to our homes to celebrate the birth of our Lord among our families, I have one last thing to share."

He reached into his pocket and took out a small, worn square of paper. It had a dirty string wrapped around it and the fold of the paper was sealed with a daub of yellow wax. It was a letter.

"Yesterday, I received this letter from a courier who was passing through Charlotte town on his way north with dispatches to Hillsboro. He actually had two letters. After learning that I was a minister of the Gospel, he asked if I knew the individuals to whom these letters were addressed. When I informed him that I did, indeed, know the addressees for both letters, he entrusted them to me for delivery. He stressed that these letters were confidential and that they were recently smuggled out of Charlestown."

A gasp of excitement traveled through the crowd. A general chatter broke out among the congregation. "Charlestown! Who would be sending letters from Charlestown?" An air of tension descended upon the church.

The Elder continued, "I delivered the first letter yesterday afternoon. The man to whom it was addressed is not a part of our church. Some of you probably know him, though … Mr. Silas Moffat."

More excited chatter erupted. William's heart climbed into his throat. He knew full well that Silas' son, Joel Moffat, was James' best friend in the entire world. The Elder held up his hands to calm the crowd.

He spoke over the murmur of their voices, "The other letter … this letter … is addressed to one of our very own."

He turned his head to John Hamilton. John's heart throbbed in his chest. He felt light-headed. He thought he might pass out.

"John Hamilton, will you please come and claim your correspondence? And if you feel led and sense the freedom to do so, once you have read the letter, please consider sharing the news from Charlestown with our brethren."

John looked at William. "Go ahead, Johnny. The letter is to you! I'm dying to know what it says!"

John rose from his bench. His legs didn't want to move, but somehow he ambled methodically and deliberately to the end of the row and made his way down the aisle. Every eye was upon him. The tension was palpable.

John finally reached the platform and joined the Elder who placed the crumpled letter into his hand. He folded the letter slightly and slid the string off and then used his fingernail to break the wax seal. He looked out into the congregation and locked eyes with his mother. Tears were streaming down her cheeks. William, sitting beside her, wept also. He could almost swear that he saw a tear in Ephraim Farr's eye. It was obvious that they all assumed the letter was a source of bad news. John smiled at his mother and then handed the letter back to the Elder.

"Sir, I don't read very well. And I'm a bit too excited to even try."

The congregation laughed nervously. His mother smiled through her tears.

John continued, "I would be honored if you would just go ahead and read the letter to all the church folk. Mama deserves to hear what it says, too."

"Are you certain, John?"

"Yes, sir. Please just get on with it."

"Very well."

The Elder handed his candle to John and took the letter in his hands. John held up both candles to give the elderly gentleman more illumination.

The old man cleared his throat and began reading:

*"Dear Mr. John Hamilton,*

*"I have not had the pleasure to make your acquaintance. I cannot share my name at this time for fear of reprisal from our*

*British occupiers. Suffice it to say that I am a woman and a Patriot and that I long for the day when our oppressors will be run back into the sea. It is my sincere hope that the news I bear in this correspondence will lift your spirits as the Christmas season draws nigh.*

*"By means that I cannot disclose I have made contact with a gentleman now housed in the prison barracks in Charlestown. His name is Joel Moffat, captured during Gates' defeat at Camden. He asked that I endeavor to inform you that your brother, James Hamilton, is alive and well and living with him in the barracks housing."*

A huge cheer erupted from the congregation. John wept openly, as did his mother. She wrapped William in her arms. Even Elder Scott wiped a tear of joy from his face as he basked in the celebration ongoing in what was ordinarily a very quiet, reserved, and conservative church body.

He waved his hands in a hopeless effort to try and calm the crowd. It was several minutes before he was able to resume reading the letter. Finally, the rowdy din dulled to an excited murmur.

"Folks, if I might continue … "

He cleared his throat again.

*"Mr. Moffat has informed me that there are several dozen men from your county's regiment who were captured on the same day as he. Many have perished from the pox, the bloody flux, and starvation, but some remain alive. Please know that their situation is dire and that the British are most harsh in their treatment. But also know that they are more determined than ever to remain alive and defiant in the face of their cruel captors.*

*"Please know also that I and others like me are attempting to send food and supplies to the men inside the camp. I will also endeavor to forward further correspondence and information to you as I have the opportunity.*

*"Please give my regards to Mrs. Farr, and let her know that her son loves her and misses her dearly. I am your humble servant, a lady and Patriot of South Carolina. God save the United States of*

*America!"*

Elder Scott placed his arm around John's shoulders and in a very uncharacteristic fashion shouted, "Now, folks, that is good news!"

The men picked up and waved their hats and broke out in cheers of, "Huzzah!"

# CHAPTER FIFTEEN

It was a harsh winter for the Hamilton brothers. Both of them caught a horrible fever shortly after Christmas. William got better from the sickness much quicker than John. In fact, John came close to death. But they both eventually recovered. It took two full months for John to feel like himself again.

In April John was called to action in the militia and had to go to South Carolina. He fought in a battle there at a place called Hobkirk's Hill, near Camden ... the place where James had been captured the previous year. John survived the battle and returned home in a matter of days.

John settled back into normal life after returning home from that battle. It was mid-May and the boys should have been in the middle of planting and farming season, but there was no seed to be found in Mecklenburg County in the spring of 1781.

Since their farm was non-producing and dormant, they stayed on the Farr property and helped Ephraim whenever they could. They would have to hold on and make do until the war was over and James came home. They hoped beyond hope that life would return to normal sometime soon.

Another letter made it through from Charlestown and broke the monotony of their day-to-day existence. It arrived on June 5, but it was dated May 22. The letter read:

*"Dear Mr. John Hamilton,*

*"It is with great joy that I write to you again to send you news of your dear brother. I apologize sincerely for the lack of correspondence over these past months. Our courier system was compromised during the winter and discovered by our common enemy. It has taken several months to re-establish a dependable network by which to forward correspondence northward.*

*"James is doing as well as can be expected. I have had regular contact with him through Mr. Moffat. I even spoke to him personally on two occasions when he ventured close enough to our normal place of rendezvous. Both men have fared well during their stay in the prisoner barracks. There is less disease and privation in the camp than on board the deathly ships in our harbor.*

*"I have managed to smuggle modest amounts of food and supplies through the fence to them. We cannot exchange much in the way of goods, though, as we do not want to betray your brother and his friend through the appearance of health that is better than that of their comrades. It is a difficult balance to find.*

*"We hold hope that there will soon be a general exchange of prisoners. Rumors abound in Charlestown regarding such a possibility, but I have no way to confirm those rumors.*

*"There is also another rumor that the camp will soon be shut down and all men moved on board prison ships. We pray that this is not the case. I trust that you will join us in that prayer.*

*"Please rest assured that if there is any change in your brother's status that I will endeavor to forward information to you at the first possible opportunity.*

*"Please give my regards to James' mother, and let her know that her son still loves her and misses her dearly. I remain your humble servant, a lady and Patriot of the free state of South Carolina. God save the United States of America."*

So John, William, their mother, and all of their family and friends prayed fervently that James would not have to serve any more time on a British prison ship.

\* \* \*

The notice arrived unexpectedly on July 4. It came by courier from Camden and points south. The sheriff posted it at the courthouse. That was the best that he could do to get the information disseminated into the community. His method worked very quickly, especially with the patriotic fervor and celebrations surrounding the fifth anniversary of the Declaration of Independence from Great Britain. Word of mouth spread quickly throughout the county and region.

The notice read:

*"By Order of General Sir Henry Clinton, Commander of His Majesty's Forces in the Americas –*

*"A most amicable agreement for the exchange of prisoners has been attained between His Majesty's forces and the armies and naval forces currently in rebellion against Great Britain. All rebel prisoners taken in the colonies of Georgia, North Carolina, South Carolina, and Virginia and being held in facilities in and around Charlestown will be exchanged forthwith on the island of Jamestown, Virginia. Such exchange to commence on July 15 and will continue until all agreed terms are met. Families wishing to redeem their family members are instructed to proceed to the point of exchange at their own leisure and expense.*

*"God save King George III."*

Daniel Pippin was breathless when he rode up to the Farr cabin in search of John and William late that evening. Daniel's brother, Henry Pippin, was a close friend of James Hamilton. He, too, was missing after the battle at Camden.

John opened the door and yawned, "What's wrong, Daniel?"

"They're being released right away! Our brothers are being released!"

"What? How do you know? Where?"

"There's a letter posted at the courthouse, just sent north from Charlestown. It says that Clinton has ordered an exchange to commence on the fifteenth of this month."

"That's less than two weeks!" exclaimed John.

"I know! That's why I came right over. We've to go get them."

"Where?"

"Jamestown."

"Virginia?" John exclaimed. "Why Virginia? Why not just let them go at Charlestown?"

"I don't rightly know. Maybe because it's an exchange. Our prison camps are all up north. Maybe its half-way in between the two of them, or something."

John nodded, "That makes sense."

"We need to get going as quick as we can. I say we light out tomorrow."

"You're probably right," John affirmed. "There's no telling how long it'll take to get there. But we need to plan a bit, though."

"What's to plan? We take plenty of food, extra clothes, and some powder and lead. We'll sort the rest out as we go."

John smiled at his friend and placed his hand on his shoulder, "Dan, you know we haven't heard a single word about Henry."

Daniel looked down at the floor, "I know, Johnny, but I can still hope. I have to, for Ma and Pa's sake, at least. But even if Henry's dead, I have to help you get James back home. That's what friends do."

John hugged his best friend.

"I'll see you in the morning, Daniel."

* * *

John awakened early the next morning and made his preparations. The entire house was thrown into an uproar by the news of the prisoner exchange.

John was floored when Ephraim sat down with him and stated his personal intentions.

"John, I aim to go to Jamestown with you."

"Me, too!" injected William.

Ephraim looked at William and started to object, but then nodded his head in agreement.

"William deserves to go, as well. James is his brother, too."

John objected, "But Mr. Farr, Daniel Pippin is already going with me. We were figuring on doing this ourselves."

Ephraim shook his head in disagreement, "I don't think that's a good idea, John. It's a long way to Jamestown … every bit of three hundred miles. There will be river crossings along the way. There might be Tories still on the loose. You need more hands and guns. Four will be better than two."

"What about the horses? That'll be a heavy load for one team, especially bringing men back with us. It might be more than James and Joel Moffat that need a ride home."

"We'll take extra horses. We'll tie on my team as a spare, and William and I will ride our own mounts."

John smiled, "Sounds like you've thought this all through."

Ephraim nodded. "Truth is, I thought this out a long time ago. I've just been waiting on the opportunity to go and get James."

"I'm grateful, Mr. Farr."

"John, I know that you'll never call me 'Pa.' I don't deserve that, at all, after the way I acted toward you boys through the years. But can you at least call me Ephraim?"

"I can do that, Ephraim."

Ephraim smiled and smacked John on the knee. "Good! Now let's eat some of your Mama's fine cooking and pack us a wagon."

# CHAPTER FIFTEEN

It was twelve days later, July 17, 1781, when the wagon and four weary riders from Mecklenburg County arrived at Swanns Point on the James River opposite Jamestown. It was a torturous journey. Because it was an unfamiliar land and terrain for them, they lost their way several times and twice had to cut cross-country in an effort to find suitable roads to reach their destination. But at long last the village was in view. There were two large ships anchored off the point and military encampments littered the far shore.

John left the other men to set up camp and hired a small boat to take him across the wide, slow-moving river. He soon found a very polite British major who had the dubious responsibility of disseminating information to people in search of their loved ones. The officer informed him that, thus far, only four ships bearing prisoners had arrived from Charlestown.

A quick survey of the passenger manifests showed that James Hamilton was not on any of those vessels. Furthermore, the British government could not give any assurances of how many ships were coming or the schedules of any possible arrivals. John returned downcast to their camp across the river.

For the next three days the men amused themselves as best they could. During the daytime they occupied their time taking naps in the shade or fishing in the brackish water. They talked, ate, and smoked their pipes. They played cards and told stories. They sought out and talked to other families waiting diligently for their sons and husbands to arrive.

The nights were miserable, for it was in the darkness that hordes of buzzing mosquitoes descended upon them. They tried everything to keep them at bay. They lit heavily smoking fires throughout their camp and covered their exposed skin with mud and ash. Still, the blood-sucking pests fought their way through and left all four of them covered with hundreds of itchy welts. Poor Daniel Pippin seemed to have excessive numbers of the bites and appeared especially sensitive to the insect's venom. The others appropriately dubbed him, "Sweet meat."

Early on the morning of the fifth day, July 21, William shocked the others from their boredom when he literally shrieked, "There's a boat coming!"

Sure enough, there was a schooner downriver. It had just rounded the point four miles to the southeast and was slowly making its way toward Jamestown.

John shot Ephraim a hopeful look.

"You boys go on over," Ephraim instructed. "I'll wait here and keep an eye on camp."

John grabbed a silver coin from his bag to pay the oarsman and the boys joined the small flotilla of tiny fishing vessels making its way northeast across the river. They pulled up on the muddy shore about ten minutes before the ship docked. People began to crowd around the point of debarkation.

A loud British captain bellowed, "Civilians will kindly stay behind the fence! Please allow us to do our work. If your family member is aboard this vessel, you will know shortly! Do not make me tell you again!"

A small detail of Redcoats pushed its way through the crowd and stationed themselves as a barrier between the family members and the dock. The crowd backed up several steps.

Moments later the ship came into clear view. Well over one hundred men crowded the rail around the deck and peered into the waiting throng of civilians. Each man, most assuredly, prayed and hoped that they had at least one loved one in the mass of people.

John strained to see the faces of the men, but they all looked the same to him. They were all bearded and filthy and dressed in little more than rags. They were a pitiful sight, indeed.

The ship soon bumped and groaned to a stop against the timbers along the dock. It rode low in the water, so the level of descent from the deck of the boat to the small wooden dock was only about eight feet. A British soldier on board kicked a rope ladder over the side. The ladder dropped and the bottom end landed on the wood platform with a loud thump. Then, one by one, the skinny, pitiful men began to come down the ladder.

The Redcoat major standing at the base of the ladder shouted, "Prisoners! As you disembark you will state your name for checking against the ship's official manifest. You will be informed whether you are dismissed or if you must wait in the holding area for further documentation or interrogation. First prisoner!"

The pitiful man at the front of the line stated plainly, "Michael Overby."

The officer marked an "x" on his paper and then stated, "Michael Overby, you are dismissed."

This ritual was repeated over and over again. Only two of the men so far had family waiting for their return. The look of want and disappointment on all the other men's faces was almost unbearable. William fought the urge to cry. He simply could not believe the emaciated state of the men. His hatred for the British burned.

Over thirty men had descended the ladder, but so far no familiar names had sounded off. John and William's disappointment grew.

William stated sadly, "James must be on another boat."

Suddenly the officer in charged blurted out, "Well, state your name, you ignorant rebel!"

"My name's Joel Moffat, you wig-wearin' sissy!"

"Watch your mouth, boy, or I'll have you run through!"

The crowd held its collective breath, not believing the insolence of this skinny, wooly mountain man. John fought his way toward the front of the crowd to try and see Joel. The officer hesitated with his response, and then marked an "x" on his paper.

"The rebel Joel Moffat is dismissed ... and good riddance! Next!"

The next emaciated man spoke, "James Hamilton."

"James Hamilton, you are dismissed."

John finally plowed his way through the crowd. His eyes met his brother's eyes. He screamed from the depths of his lungs and his soul, "Jamie!"

James didn't run to him. He couldn't. He could barely shuffle his feet. But he finally made his way past the Redcoat guards. John reached out to him and picked his big brother up in his arms in a tremendous bear hug. Unbelievably, John Hamilton now outweighed his elder brother by at least fifty pounds.

The crowd cheered at their emotional reunion. They parted to allow William and Daniel through. William took hold of his big brother and wept.

"What about me?" ask the smiling Joel Moffat who stood nearby watching the entire spectacle.

The Hamilton boys pulled him into their huddle, as well. Only Daniel Pippin stood alone. He peered anxiously at the men who continued to climb slowly down the ladder from the prison ship.

James reached over and took Daniel by the arm, pulling

him near. He grabbed the boy behind the back of his neck and pulled him close, looking him directly in the eyes.

"Daniel, he's not coming."

Daniel nodded, tears welling in his eyes. "I didn't think so. We haven't heard from anyone but you and Joel these past months."

"Daniel, your brother was our best good friend. He took sick right after we arrived on the first prison ship and died a few weeks later. He died peacefully in his sleep. He just went to sleep one night and didn't wake up."

"That's the honest truth, Daniel," affirmed Joel.

James continued, "We volunteered for the burial detail the next day. Joel and I buried him. We picked a pretty spot on the beach and we marked it in our minds. We know where he lays. Maybe we can take you there one of these days. Would you like for us to do that, maybe?"

Daniel nodded in silent response. James pulled the boy close and hugged him.

After a few more minutes of celebration, John spoke up, "Why don't we get on back across the river. I don't like being around all these Lobsterbacks."

"Amen to that, Johnny!" exclaimed Joel as the group made their way to their small hired boat.

William and John helped support James as they walked across the hard rock and shells. Daniel helped Joel, but the sharp surface didn't seem to bother him as much.

William told James as they walked, "Ephraim is waiting for us across the river."

James stopped in his tracks and looked at John. He exclaimed, "Ephraim Farr?"

John smiled and kept walking. "I'll tell you all about it, brother. Right now we need to get you two on over to the other side and get hold of some soap and razors. You both smell like a skunk died under your armpits!"

"Two skunks, at least!" chirped William.

The young men howled with laughter.

One hour later James and Joel bathed in the brackish

water of the James River. Ephraim boiled some fresh water and gave them both a much-needed shave. He had to sharpen his razor three times to cut through their matted beards.

James watched his stepfather closely as he patiently shaved his face. It was hard to believe that the man who had been so mean to him for so many years, and was the object of his hatred for so long, was now showing him such mercy and kindness.

While Ephraim took care of their hair problems and helped make them more socially presentable, the other boys burned their nasty, vermin-filled clothes and laid out fresh breeches, socks, shirts, and weskits for them both. William provided them each with a beautiful set of moccasins that he made from elk hide.

Then they ate. Both men tried to eat too much at first, but Ephraim insisted that they proceed carefully in order to not become sick from overstuffing their shrunken stomachs. The men paced themselves, eating small meals and snacks, almost without ceasing. They ate and relaxed for two whole days along the river as their strength slowly found its way back into their members.

On the third morning after James and Joel were released, Ephraim and the boys awakened to find James and Joel breaking camp and loading their gear into the wagon.

James stated plainly and simply, "It's time to go home."

"The Redcoats burned our cabin and barn, James. We don't have a home, anymore," replied William.

James walked over to his little brother. "William, my home is where you are. It's where Johnny is. My brothers are my home."

William smiled and responded, "Then I'm ready. Let's go home … together."

And they did. James, Johnny, and William Hamilton's war was over.

Three months later George Washington slipped down

from the north and the French fleet sailed into Chesapeake Bay and cornered General Cornwallis just twenty miles to the east of Jamestown at a place called Yorktown, Virginia. And Cornwallis surrendered.

The American Revolution was over. The United States of America won its freedom and independence. And the Hamilton brothers went back to Mecklenburg County, rebuilt their cabin, and finally found peace.

# THE REAL HAMILTON BROTHERS

Though some of the characters in this story are fictional, most of them were real, historical individuals. James, John, William, and Hugh Hamilton were all the sons of Hugh Hamilton of Mecklenburg County. They have many descendants living today. Both the Sons and Daughters of the American Revolution recognize James and John Hamilton as Patriots of the American Revolution.

James Hamilton served in the militia in Mecklenburg County. His service is described in detail in his federal pension file in the National Archives. In that record he offered testimony regarding his actual battles and his capture at Camden, as well as his imprisonment on a British ship in Charleston.

John Hamilton served the Patriot cause, as well. He received payment for providing supplies to the cause and for service in the militia. The records for those transactions are located in the North Carolina state archives. However, the details of his actual service during the war are lost to time. Suffice it to say that he was, indeed, a Patriot and a soldier in the American Revolution.

William Hamilton's service in the American Revolution is not documented. However, thousands of young men his age served in the American armies and performed Patriotic Service in support of the United States. This story about William is fiction, but we can rest assured that he was a Patriot from a dedicated family of Patriots.

*Geoff Baggett*

# REVOLUTIONARY WAR GLOSSARY

**Charlestown** – The colonial name of Charleston.

**Continental Army** – Soldiers in the federal army of the United States as authorized by the Continental Congress.

**Dragoons** – A special type of cavalry soldier in the British army.

**Flintlock** – The type of weapons, loaded through the muzzle, used during the American Revolution.

**Frizzen** – The part of a flintlock weapon that the flint strikes to make a spark and ignite the gunpowder.

**Huzzah** – A joyful shout, and the early form of the modern word, "hoorah," or "hooray."

**Loyalist** – A citizen of the American colonies loyal to King George III and Great Britain.

**Militia** – Local county and state military units. Most served locally. There were both Patriot and Loyalist militia units during the war.

**Muster** – The official forming of local militia units for mobilization in the war.

**Patriots** – People in American who were in favor of separation from England and the formation of a separate country.

**Redcoats** – The name that Patriots called British soldiers.

**Tory / Tories** – Another name for Loyalists.

**Waxhaws** – The name given to a geographical region along the borders of North and South Carolina just south of Charlotte.

# ABOUT THE AUTHOR

Geoff Baggett is a small town pastor in rural Kentucky. Though his formal education and degrees are in the fields of chemistry, biology, and Christian theology, his hobbies and obsessions (according to his wife) are genealogy and Revolutionary War history. He is an active member of the Sons of the American Revolution and has discovered over twenty Patriot ancestors in his family tree from the states of Virginia, North and South Carolina, and Georgia.

Geoff is an avid living historian, appearing regularly in period uniform in classrooms, reenactments, and other Revolutionary War commemorative events throughout the southeastern United States. He lives on a small piece of land in rural Trigg County, Kentucky, with his amazing wife, a daughter and grandson, and a yard full of fruit trees and perpetually hungry chickens and goats.

54911953R10062

Made in the USA
Charleston, SC
18 April 2016